RUN AND TELL THAT

KAREN BRISCO

authorHOUSE®

AuthorHouse™
1663 Liberty Drive
Bloomington, IN 47403
www.authorhouse.com
Phone: 1-800-839-8640

Published by AuthorHouse   05/03/2012

ISBN: 978-1-4685-7171-4 (sc)
ISBN: 978-1-4685-7170-7 (e)

Library of Congress Control Number: 2012908123

Any people depicted in stock imagery provided by Thinkstock are models, and such images are being used for illustrative purposes only.
Certain stock imagery © Thinkstock.

This book is printed on acid-free paper.

Because of the dynamic nature of the Internet, any web addresses or links contained in this book may have changed since publication and may no longer be valid. The views expressed in this work are solely those of the author and do not necessarily reflect the views of the publisher, and the publisher hereby disclaims any responsibility for them.

TABE OF CONTENTS

PREFACE

Run and Tell That is a book of short stories that is breathtaking and heart pounding. You won't be able to put it down. Some stories may cause you to get angry, or even cause you to have hope again; hold on to your seats. Stay still—inhale, exhale. One thing is for sure; many people will be able to relate to one of these stories, be it good or bad.

The main thing is, don't take offense; think about it, and twirl it around in your head. Think about the secrets that someone you know has shared with you, the stories you heard from friends and family, and things that have happened to some of them. Believe it or not, one of these stories just may be yours, and if it is, don't worry, I got you! I will tell it just like it is! Maybe this may cause the abuser to stop the abuse, or the liars to stop lying.

There are men and women out there that have so much dirt in their backyards that you can't see the grass. To the mothers and fathers, pay close attention to your kids. To husbands and wives, stop lying to each other; it is what is. Communicate, and don't be afraid of what he or she may say. Knowing is a beginning of moving forward toward dealing with whatever situations you face. Grow up people; you have the right to choose how you want to live your life. It's all about choices! Let's learn how to stop spinning our wheels, and know life goes on; you win some and lose some. Life has never been fair, and don't go around thinking that is it. Just be true to yourself and your good. In this world, we have freedom of speech, freedom of choice, and the right to be happy.

The first story is dedicated to my loving nephew,
Lu'Mon William Brisco. May he rest in peace.

I CALLED HIM MY ANGEL

Lu'Mon William Brisco, who was nine years old, was born in mid—November with the prettiest smile you have ever seen. When he was a baby he didn't cry that much—only when he was hungry. Growing up he played by himself a lot. I had nothing but love for him, I gave him everything I could, and he knew it; we had faith and hope on our side.

My Lu'Mon William would tell me, "Mom, when I get rich I'm going to buy you a house, with a great big swimming pool in the backyard."

I would say, "Okay, baby."

Years passed, and we moved out of state to live with one of my sisters; there he ran track and sang in the school choir. Time went on, and Lu'Mon was worrying me to move back home. Well, I didn't like it there anyway. I took him out of school and returned to our hometown to live. No matter what the situation was, my Lu'Mon would hold his head high, proud, just like I taught him to be.

He had a baby brother he was very fond of. He also had cousins, but most of them live out of the state where he had just moved from. Boy, was he crazy about his cousins. He enjoyed saying "my cousins." My Lu'Mon was so proud of his last name; he played baseball, and everybody loved him. An old friend of mine from the same neighborhood we lived in would visit us from time to time, nothing serious, but he was Lu'Mon's best buddy. At that point in my life, I didn't want anything to do with a man. I always kept it on a friendship level. Going to church every Sunday, prayer meetings and everything, bible study, you name it, Lu'Mon William and I were there. One thing we did a lot of was praying. It had been about a year after we returned home, and Lu'Mon William was in school making new friends, and he joined the baseball team. Practice was every evening after school. I would take him and wait on the bench or in the car for him. He was a proud first baseman and pitcher, and, boy, was he great at his job. Their team was undefeated, and they were headed to the playoffs. This was the most excitement my son had ever been a part of. His best buddy, now my close friend, began to come out to the baseball field to watch Lu'Mon practice; we would talk and laugh for hours. Then one day before we knew it, he had somehow became a baseball coach. So now after practice we would sometimes go and get something to eat together; Lu'Mon sure did like that. No one knew but me and Lu'Mon, about our hard times and how we didn't have enough food to eat at times. I can recall this one time I had only one can of beans to feed my son, and no gas to cook them with. My Lu'Mon sat right there on the floor in our half-empty apartment and ate those raw beans; that was truly my lowest.

My angel ate up those beans like it was a gourmet meal and had a smile on his face. When I would look at him, in his eyes I could see he knew and understood just where we were but had enough strength to encourage me that things were fine, and he would just smile at me and melt my heart away.

As time went on things got better; my brother would come over to visit us from time to time. We had friends from church, and Lu'Mon's buddy would come over to take him to baseball practice; he called him his best buddy. Lu'Mon wasn't too sure if he wanted me to have a boyfriend, so he would ask me when a guy would speak to me, "Momma, who is that?" But as his love grew for his best buddy he started to ask me more questions about why I didn't like his best buddy. I would look at him and laugh, but I knew in my heart he was really serious about his love for this guy and about how he wanted him to be his daddy. One night while we were in bed he said, "Momma, marry my buddy and make him my daddy." Well I didn't let Lu'Mon know, but I began to see his best buddy in a different light. Here it was: this man, who was everything I needed for my son and who was so kind, loving, and gentle to us both, I had fallen for him.

Finally his dreams were coming true. But the very next month my angel, our angel, was gone. Lu'Mon was a great student in school, and he had received a Super Citizen Award for the end of the school year, and they were going on a field trip and, boy, did he want to go. I had decided to let my Lu'Mon go on this field trip without me.

They had decided to have a special party just for the Super Citizens; they took them swimming, but something went wrong. They had left the kids there unsupervised; all I was told was when they got back they saw a lil boy lying next to a fence. He was lifeless and soaking wet, dead, never to hear his voice again. I will never know what happened on that day; all in one moment my whole life as I knew it for nine years was gone. The next year I married his best buddy, just as he said I would. I often wonder if he knew that this was the man for me. Of course he did, and he's watching over us now. I love you, Lu'Mon William Brisco, and you will never be forgotten.

Your brother told me, "Mom, my brother came to me last night and told me that I could have his baseball glove. I said, 'Really?' Yeah, momma, he told me I could have it. Momma, Lu'Mon was smiling. He told me he was playing with a lot of kids, and then he went away."

Who am I to tell my two-year-old son that he didn't see his brother? After all, love never dies. It lives on in our hearts, so from time to time we stop and remember his love, his touch, and his smile.

May you rest in peace, my angel.

YOUNG AND TENDER

Here I am, a middle-aged black female, finding herself often wondering about younger men. What's it like? Will someone find out if I test the waters? The craziest thing about it is they keep looking back. One cold winter night I was over at my girlfriend's house getting my head bad.

Her doorbell rings; she answers. Standing in her door were two tall, handsome black males. I mean young, about in their early twenties. One of them was a friend of hers; now I remember her telling me about this young guy that she gets with sometimes, but I had never seem him. Well, the two of them came in, and the other person caught my eyes. He kept looking at me and making jokes, and that night turned into a night to remember. Stacey, my girlfriend, and I had a great time that night, Jeffery, Stacey's friend, took her in the room, and that left me and Robert alone in the living room. Well, we began to play around with each other, which led to kissing and heavy petting, if you know what I mean. It got so hot I told him that I was getting ready to leave, and he said he was too. We both yelled into the bedroom to the others that we were leaving; they told us to make sure we locked the door. We kissed again; I gave him my number, and he gave me his. The next evening he called.

"What a big surprise!"

"Why?"

"I did not expect you to really use that number."

"Well, I did. Are you disappointed?"

"No, actually I am very pleased. I was just thinking about you."

"Oh, really?"

"Yes, really. How is your day going?"

"Great, since I heard your voice."

Smiling, I said, "Well, that is a good thing."

We got off the phone, and I wondered if he wanted to see me again. We didn't make plans or anything, but just knowing that he was feeling me was even better. Well, late that night I called him, and he was alone and sounding so sexy. I began to talk a little dirty to him; he responded with more dirty talk, and before we knew it we were both hot and horny. We climaxed over the phone; it was crazy, but it felt so good. All I could think about at that moment was what his face looked like when he was yelling. I told him, "Damn, I wish you were here sounding like that." He replied by saying, "Me too, baby." We said good night, and, ooh, did I sleep well.

The phone sex went on about a month. One evening I invited Robert over for a nice dinner; I had baked fish, fresh vegetables, steamed rice, and a nice bottle of wine. I made it very nice. We both enjoyed dinner; afterward I took him to the living room, put on some nice jazz and told him to relax, saying, "I will be right back." I went into the bedroom and put on the sexiest thing I could find. I called him to my bedroom door. Robert looked at me in a way that made me want him even more; he walked toward me and picked me up off the floor. He began to kiss me wildly, laying me on the bed. I did not have to lead him to anything; he found every spot on his own. His touch was as if he had been there before. Robert slept over that night; he made breakfast. We got in the shower together and had more hot sex. I was trying not to think too much into this and just enjoying what was happening and going with the flow. Robert asked me to go to the beach later, and that's what we did. We had lunch on the beach and went over to his place. My girlfriend Stacy called me on my cell, asking me what I was doing that day. "Girl, I'm over here at Robert's house."

"Robert's house? "Girl, go ahead."

I told her I would talk to her later. About an hour later Jeffery called Robert's phone. Jeffery was asking Robert the same thing, and Robert told him that he had company, and it was me. Jeffery said, "Well, I am going to pick up Stacy. Is it alright if we come over?" Robert held the phone and asked me if I minded if they intrude. "Whatever. I don't care," I said. Robert said, "Sure, you guys come on." When they got there we had put some meat on the grill; he got the cards out. Robert had a patio. Jeffery and Stacy just watched us having a good time together, and then they started in on us. Here come the comments, such as, "Boy, are we having fun. Can you sit any closer?" After everything was out in the open, things really began to pick up. We began to see each other at least four days out of a week, and sometimes more than that. Things seemed to get serious between us; I was falling for him and did not want him to know it. He knew that I was holding back; he just didn't say anything.

One night we were having great sex. He asked me if I would consider moving into his place.

"Wouldn't it be nice if we could wake up with each other?"

I asked him, "Where is all that coming from?"

He said that he wanted to talk to me about something.

"Go ahead."

"Thelma, I'm in love with you."

Things got quiet in the room.

"What's wrong? Did I say the wrong thing? How do you feel about what I just said?"

I asked him how he knew he was in love with me.

He paused for a moment and said, "There's so many things I love about you, Thelma. First of all, I love your presence, just being in the same room with you. I love the way you look at me, the way you talk to me, and the consideration you have for me. The way you respond to my touch. Thelma, I may be younger, but what difference does that make? You can be unhappy with a man your age or even older. I know that having you in my life makes me smile in the morning when I get up to get ready for work. At night, I find myself rolling in the bed searching for your smell in the sheets. I love you, Thelma, and if you don't want to live with me it's okay. I just wanted you to know how I feel about you. The feeling I have is as if the other half of me has finally arrived. Do you have anything to say about my confession?"

"Robert, I am glad that you feel the way you do about me. I can truly say that I have been having the best time of my life; I must tell you that I am afraid of starting all over again. I know that the feeling is there, and the sex is good. Now here it comes. But the next man I live with will be my husband."

"Oh I heard that, loud and clear."

After that we did not talk about living together anymore. When women mention marriage that usually run men away. Whatever happens will separate the men from the boys. Robert and I continued to see each other, and we got closer and closer. Now I am in love trying to hide it because I don't want him to get the big head. Two days later Stacy called and asked if Robert and I wanted to go to Palm Springs for the weekend with her and Jeffery, and we said yes. On the way, we stopped at the rest area. Two women in a car were laughing and talking; one of them called Jeffery to their car to ask for directions to Palm Springs. They thought that they were going the wrong way. Whatever, on that! Well, Jeffery told them that we were going the same way, and they could follow us. When Jeffery got in the car Stacy asked him what that was all about. He told her the women were lost, and they were going to follow us to Palm Springs. Stacy looked at me, and I looked at Robert. Okay, on to Palm Springs. That night we were all sitting in the lounge of the resort, and Robert goes, "Hey, there's those women that followed us from the rest stop. Oh boy, here they come."

The tall, skinny blonde said, "Looks like you guys are having fun."

Looking out the corner of my eye, I could see her watching my Robert. I didn't say anything, but I kept my eyes on her. They asked if they could join us.

Stacy said, "Hell no. You followed us here. That was good enough; if there's one thing we don't need it is your company."

Jeffery told her that Stacy wasn't nice, and to stop being so hateful. "We didn't come out here for this; we came to enjoy each other," he said. Jeffery insisted that they stay.

I told Robert, "It's time to go to our room."

Robert said, "Let's go."

My man followed my lead without me having to explain why. I knew that I could let him in more and that he was the man for me.

At that point, Robert had begun to read me. He knew my body language, and he was able to look at me and tell when I was uncomfortable; he just knew. We both knew that this was heading for trouble. Robert and I were having a good time, but Stacy and Jeffery had company for the whole weekend. When we got home, I asked Stacy, "What was that all about? What is up with Jeffery, and does he have the white woman fever?

"Yes."

"And you're okay with that?

"He's not my man or anything; I don't give a damn."

"He's with you now. Being your man has nothing to do with respecting you."

Stacy said, "Girl, I don't care. As long as he's not my man, I don't care."

"You should care. You were the one he was disrespecting, and if you don't realize how awful that made you look, you're in bad shape. A man only does what you let him; if you are going to continue to see him I advise you to talk to him. You need to demand your respect. That's why some white women do what they do. That white bitch had already checked your man out and knew that they could get away with that bullshit. When those two women called Jeffery to the car, he ran so fast; they knew then. Stacy, you are good, because it could not be me. You have to check those tricks at the door, your friend allowed her to disrespect you."

"Disrespect me? How did they disrespect me?"

"If you don't know, Stacy, you never will."

Stacy stopped talking to me for a while. Time went on, and I called Stacy. I missed her friendship; I could tell she was happy to hear from me. We talked about the whole thing again. She said she thought about it, and that's why he'd been what he was to her, a friend.

"I would not call him a friend, because friends respect each other. Not trying to get on your bad side again, Stacy, but I want you to know that you are a good person with a lot of qualities. Stop laughing at everything Jeffery does, because the joke is on you. Men sense the old days do what they want and how they want, without being judged by others. We, on the other hand, as females have to be very careful of the things we say and do. Not that it's fair, but that is the law of the land. Well, Stacy, you know that I love you. I am sharing these things with you because I care, and I have been through a couple of things myself. You know I don't have to tell you that I would never purposely disrespect you or hurt your feelings. I wouldn't be a friend if I didn't tell you the truth. Jeffery knows I don't care that much about him, but it isn't my call; it's yours."

Stacy replied, "Well, enough about this. How are you and Robert getting along? You guys seem serious."

"We are serious, Stacy interrupts saying, Ms. I will never date a younger man. Yeah, never say never."

She laughed. Who would have thought that I would be here doing this? I had always said that I would never date anyone younger than me; however, look at me now. I am wide open and loving it. I had decided to step out on faith with Robert and give it a try. As the days went on, I found myself looking and waiting for something to go wrong, and it did. Robert called me and told me that his job was going to lay off people, and he didn't know how it would affect him.

I told him, "Don't worry. God is on your side."

Later that day he said, "You see, Thelma, that's what I'm talking about. You always have something positive to say; you always seem to calm me. I would never take you for granted."

"You know, Robert, I feed off the way you treat me, the kind words you say, how you speak to me, and how you watch what you say or do in front of me. I could never take you for granted."

"November is here, and we are getting ready for Thanksgiving; our families are involved. "Thelma, I would like you to meet my parents."

Thelma. You will love my parents; I know I will. They are so excited to meet you; I told them all about you."

We began to make plans. He called his parents, and we decided to go to Atlanta for Thanksgiving. That night Robert slept at my place. I asked Robert if he wanted kids.

He said, "I really don't know how to answer that."

"What do you mean, you don't know how to answer that."

"Well, baby, I know that you are at the age where you are not thinking about children anymore. It's not that I don't want children; it just never happened for me. I never considered kids before because of previous relationships; however, if you want kids you still have time; you are still young, Thelma."

"What does that mean? If you cannot have kids I don't want any."

"Just because I cannot have your children doesn't mean you don't deserve to have kids, Thelma."

"What are you saying? Robert, can we talk about this later?"

"No, why later?"

I started crying.

"Thelma, why are you crying?" He was holding me in his arms.

I cannot believe that God has blessed me with this man after all this time, and I cannot have his children. Why am I sending myself through this? We are not married.

"There's still time for you, Robert. After we come from Atlanta we need to talk about our future together."

"We can talk about it all we want Thelma, but I'm telling you now, I not giving you up. I have waited a long time for a love like yours."

Looking him in his eyes while he was holding me, I could feel everything he was saying.

"It wouldn't be fair to ask you to give up something you deserve; you deserve to have your own child. Look, let's not talk about this right now, please."

Things got quiet, and we both fell asleep. The next morning Robert got up first; he was in the kitchen cooking. The smell woke me up. I went into the kitchen. Robert kissed me long and hard. What was that about?

"I love you. I need you in my life, right beside me, and I need you to tell me that you feel the same way."

"Robert, you know I do."

"But without all the buts. We love each other, and if you don't want to have a baby at your age fine; I'm good with that. I have you right now, not a baby. When I met you it wasn't a secret you were older than me. You make me happy. Sure, if by chance you were to have my baby, great. But I fell in love with Thelma. Can't you understand that? Thelma, will you marry me?"

I fell to my knees. He stood me up, tears rolling down my face.

"Thelma, I have never been so sure of anything in my life, and this is a sure thing, you and me."

Kissing me on my face, my eyes, nose, ears, and chin, he's whispering softly, "Thelma, can you feel me? I'm speaking from my heart. Listen."

"Yes, I feel you."

"Well, tell me you'll marry me."

"No."

He looked at me and I said, "I don't see any rock in your hand."

Enough said, he gave me a soft kiss, and we began to eat breakfast. After breakfast I told Robert I was going home and to not forget to call his parents tomorrow and tell them our traveling arrangements.

"Okay, I will see you tomorrow."

When I got home, I called Stacy for small talk. She was at home crying. I asked her what was wrong.

She told me, "You will never believe what happened to me."

"What, Stacy, what?"

"I am pregnant."

"What? Pregnant by whom?"

"Eric."

"Who is Eric?"

"Eric is the man that I am in love with. We have been sleeping around for about three years, and that is not all."

"What, girl, what?

"He is married."

"Stacy, no. You know better."

"I know, Thelma. I have tried too many times to stop seeing him, but I can't. I love him, and I have already accepted him being married."

"Stacy, why is this my first time hearing about him?"

"Because I didn't want to be judged."

"No, that is not why. Your ass knew it was wrong; now look at you. What is next?"

"I don't know."

"Yeah, you know. Are you going to keep the baby?"

She said (yelling), "What kind of question is that?"

"Just what I said. But you don't have to answer. I see that look in your eyes; you want this baby."

"Yes, I do. Anything that is a part of him I want. This is not my first time pregnant by Eric. The first time I had an abortion; his wife cannot have kids for him."

When she said that, a light bulb went off in my head. The first thing I thought about was Robert and me; we had just talked about him having kids. My heart started beating fast. I got so scared I stop talking to Stacy. I told her I had to go.

I began to think, "What if something like that would happen to us? What would I do?"

That night Robert called. "Hey, what's up?"

"Where are you?"

"What's wrong? You don't sound right."

"Are you coming over?"

"On my way."

Finally Robert got there. He gave me a big kiss on the forehead. "What's wrong, baby?"

"I called Stacy earlier, and she was upset. She told me that she was pregnant."

"That's great for Jeffery."

"No."

"For whom?"

"Eric."

"Who is that?"

"Apparently, she has been sleeping with him for years. She told me she was in love with him."

"What?"

"And that's not all. He's married and has no kids; his wife cannot have any."

Holding his hand together, he looked at me and said, "Don't you start, Thelma. This has nothing to do with us."

"I know, but can you see what can happen? If we were to get married . . .

"Stop, stop, already. Enough. That is Stacy and her life. Now this is what happens when you live the kind of life Stacy lives. When I am a married man, I will be just that, a married man."

He began to change the conversation, saying, "Thelma, are you finished packing for Atlanta?

"Yes, are you?"

"Yes. What are we eating tonight?"

"How about pizza?"

"Sounds good to me."

Next evening we left for Atlanta. We arrived in Atlanta at noon the next day, and his father was there at the airport to pick us up. He was very pleasant. We got to Robert's family house; his cousins from other parts of the country were there. Everyone was excited about seeing each other. I felt right at home; his family was down to earth people. His mother took well to me. We talked about Robert and I. She knew that I was older than Robert, and she shared a secret that Robert was keeping from me. He said he was saving this just so his mother could share her story with me. She took me in the other room, and we both sat down. She held my hand and said, "I know that my son loves you. I can hear it in his voice when he talks about you, and I have never seen him so excited about anyone. Robert has shared something with me. I want to tell you a true story; I spent most of my young life going to school. I kept focused on what I wanted, and that was to become an interior designer. I met Robert's father about one year before I finished college. His dad was still in college and had three years left. A nice-looking black man who knew how to carry himself, you couldn't tell his age by looking at him or by his conversation. We became close friends, but I had never asked him how old he was; he just looked to be my age. Little did I know that he was three years younger than I was. Yeah, that's right. Robert's father is younger than I am, and we have been married for thirty-three years. Thelma, I have raised my son not to waste time on things that don't matter. What matters to Robert is you. I love the way my son smiles, and the laughter; he is so happy, and if by chance you are the reason, I welcome you into my home, and into my heart. Please don't break his heart; stay true to each other and always talk to one another. Let him know when he hurts you; never stop doing what you are doing right now, loving and trusting in each other. Believe me, it doesn't have to stop. Love is a book of never-ending stories, some good, some bad, some beautiful, some sad, but the book of stories that Robert's father and I share, I wouldn't change or take anything away."

It was Christmas, and Robert proposed to me, and we were married the following year. We moved closer to his parents; life is good. Robert came home from work, and we both decided on baked chicken for dinner. While cooking we started talking about kids. I told Robert I had been thinking about something. He asked what.

"What about adopting kids?"

"Thelma, I know you think that I've been cheated out of having kids, but I'm not. I know you think I need to have kids. Baby, how many times do I have to tell you all I need is you?"

Thelma says, Listen, this is something we can be a part of together, Roberts replied, huh? Like what raising kids.

"Thelma, is this what you really want?"

"Yes."

"Okay, I don't want you to tell me later that I needed this to be complete. Remember, this is something that you want. I'm telling you, Thelma, we don't have to do this. I'm complete; I have you. Check into it, get as much information as you can, and check out all of our options on ways to adopt children."

"Robert, let's call your parents and tell them what we are thinking about doing. Let's hear what they think about our idea. Maybe they will have some information on adopting children."

"Sure, call them."

His mother answered the phone. I told her we were on our way over. "We have something to discuss with you and Dad."

She asked if everything was all right. I told her everything was fine. "See you when we get there."

I turned to look at Robert while on the phone with his mom; he had the biggest smile on his face. "Robert, why are you looking at me like that?"

"Why, the way you communicate with my parents means more to me than anything. Thank you, baby. It's going to be great."

Robert looked at me and asked me if I remembered the time I asked him how did he know that he loved me. "Thelma I can feel you in my heart. You didn't have to include my parents in this decision, but you did."

The next week Robert's mother and I called a couple of agencies. I got an appointment for the following week. Robert and I were nervous. We were hoping to adopt two kids, a boy and a girl. The night before we went to the agency Robert's father and mother came over to pray with us; the next day we went to the agency. We found out there are several steps you must complete before any type of adoption. The adoption process was very emotional, time consuming, and frustrating. We picked up literature here and there on adopting. One of the pamphlets we received said that more Caucasian babies are available for adoption in comparison with the number of families who want to adopt. However, there are many children of color, older children, children with special needs, and children from other countries that need families who can love and care for them. We filled out the application and had life scans done. The process became overwhelming; we were just about to give up when the agency called with good news. Our paper had been approved. "What is the next step?" I asked.

"Well, we have a young mother with a set of twins, and she has filled out papers to put these babies up for adoption. A boy and a girl."

Our eyes lit up.

"Really?"

"This mother lives on the other side of town."

"Can we talk to her? What nationality are the babies?"

"African descent."

I had all these questions in my head I wanted to ask. The agent said that I had to wait. She had to speak to the mother and let her know that she had found a family that was interested. That night we went home and prayed about it. We knew we had a long road ahead of us, but things were looking good., three months passed, the agency called and said that the babies were ours.

Robert and I went to parenting classes and childbirth classes with the mother and everything. Finally it was time for her to have the babies; she called us when it was time for her to go to the hospital. It took her about four hours before the babies were born. She let us name them. The boy we called Cobey and the girl Star. We called Robert's parents to the hospital; it was time to take the babies home from the hospital. Wow, we couldn't be any happier. Things were good between us, and life was great. The babies were growing and doing fine, but little did I know my husband had a secret. Robert confessed to me that he had a one-night stand. I was so upset; I asked him how he could let that happen.

"Baby I'm so sorry. It was the night I went bowling with the fellows. We were drinking, and the women came over to bowl with us. One thing led to another. I promise it only happen one time."

I left the room, ran into the bathroom, and locked the door. I cried so much. Robert was too ashamed to come into the same room with me. He could not even look me in the face, much less talk to me. This went on for about a week. He told his parents what he had done. They called to talk to me. I asked if I could come over alone. I arrived at his parents' house to find his mother standing in the door waiting for me. She hugged me very tightly, took my hand, and we walked around the house to the backyard. We sat down on some patio chairs; I asked her if Dad was home. No, but he would be back later, I was told.

"I wanted to talk with you first alone."

"Thelma, first I want you to talk and I'm going to listen."

She let me talk and cry on her shoulders, the whole nine yards, and then she spoke, "Thelma, I know it hurts, and it hurts bad. I want you to tell me, how bad is it?"

I looked at her and asked, "What kind of question is that?"

"Only you know how much damage he has done."

"To tell you the truth, Mom, I don't really know. All I know is that at this moment right now, with all the hurt I feel, I still love him. He told me that he would never hurt me, but he did."

"In this life, things will happen. Thelma, do you remember when I told you about my love book of never-ending stories? This is just one of the stories in your book. For, you see, I am Robert's mother; it is up to you on how you want to handle this. I know you're hurting right now. The fight comes in trying to forgive him. The question is, "Do you want to?"

"I'm so confused, only about one thing."

Mom asked what.

"On how to punish him."

She laughed so hard that I begin to laugh too. Robert's mom gave me a big kiss and told me I'd be fine. Weeks went by with Robert still walking around telling me he was sorry every chance he got. I had his ass on eggshells. I knew one thing; it was going to take more than a one-night stand to break up my happy home, and I was getting ready to make the devil out a liar. Robert and I took one day at a time, raising our kids and loving on each other.

A lot of time went by, and I decided to call Stacy to see how things were going with her and Eric. She just had a baby for a married man. She told me that Eric would come over and that he was real excited about the baby. Now get this; he told his wife about the baby, and mind you she can't have him any kids, but supposedly she was happy about the baby too. Eric told Stacy that he wasn't going to leave his wife, because he was still in love with her. I told Stacy she had better be careful; that sounds a little strange. With the drama, I had forgotten to tell her about my mine. I told her what Robert had done. Boy, did she sound happy that I had drama in my life.

"No, girl. I just know that all men are alike."

"No, I don't think so."

Stacy asked, "Thelma, what's so different about your man?"

"You mean besides being my man? He's my husband. We belong to each other. I don't have to sneak around with him. Stacy, I knew you would hate on me because I always have something to say about your men, but it's okay. I will talk to you later. My husband is home."

I forgave my husband and moved on. Stacy was in and out of court fighting for her baby. She was under investigation—too many men in and out of her house. He had pictures and everything. Eric and his wife ended up taking the baby from her, for she was considered an unfit mother.

I PROMISED YOU NOTHING

Chapter One

Men with no compassion, no self-control, are all around us. Ladies, beware of the walking heartaches. These are unsure men who are very good at what they do, unstable in all their ways. In the late '60s, I was in love and was planning my wedding. I had everything, in love with the man of my dreams. We were married in August 1968; we lived with his parents for about one year before we got our own place. Alex worked very hard, and he changed jobs all the time, trying to find one that would really support us. From the very beginning of our marriage, his mother would tell me about his ex-girlfriend name Sadie, who Alex was dating before he met me. Well, she told me that on the day we were married Sadie called to speak to Alex. His mother told her that he was getting married that day, and not to call back.

Two months later, I was pregnant. Alex began to stay out all night long with his friends, bringing home barbeque, thinking that would stop me from asking him where he had been. After the first baby it got worse; there were more women. There were women calling the house all the time, not to mention people seeing him with other women. Me pregnant, fighting with the other women. I couldn't believe what was happening before my very own eyes. I asked Alex why he lied and why he married me. He said, "Because my mother liked you so much."

I said, "What? Why are you lying? We were in love."

"No, you were in love."

I sat down in the chair and just cried.

The next week he was gone; he moved out of state. There I was with four kids, no husband, and no money. I got on welfare, which was the only way I could feed my kids. Time went on, and he began to call and ask if the kids could come to see him. He would send them money every once in a while. But nothing steady. The kids went to visit from time to time. Alex began to call me, apologizing for what he'd done, leaving me to raise the kids by myself. He asked me to move to Ohio with him; he had a house and a good job. I didn't know what to say. I just listened. All I could think was, "He's sick and dying, and now he wants me to take care of him."

All kinds of thoughts were running through my head. He told me that he changed; he was a new man now, and went to church every Sunday. I didn't answer him right away, so he began to call every day. The next time he called, I told him, "Listen, Alex, you say you've changed, you go to church and all that, but what about your habit of chasing women—the need to have several women in your life? What about what you told me when I asked you why you married me? Remember what you said? You stood right in my face and told me that your mother liked me so much, and that's why you married me. I felt so small, and felt like my heart just burst open. Now you're asking me to move away from my home. Alex, I married you because I was in love with you. We shared our dreams together. How long had you been sleeping around?

"Peggy, stop. It doesn't matter now, I made a lot of mistakes. Now I'm asking you to forgive me."

"Alex, I was lost when you left. Your mother and father did what they could for me, but I was on my own. You say none of that matters now, but it does."

I needed these questions answered for myself. Alex told me that he was just trying to hurt me when he said those things and that he has always loved me. When he was talking, I really didn't feel like he was telling the truth. In my head I was thinking. "What's really behind all this?" He came back to Tennessee to pick up the kids on vacation, and I couldn't even look him in his face. I told him the kids' bags were already packed. The kids spent the whole summer with him. They came back with school clothes and stories about where they went, and about their new friends.

"Mom, you should come with us next time."

Alex begged me to come back to him. The following month, I talked with my sister and told her that I was considering moving to Ohio with Alex. She asked me why. My sister told me she didn't think that was a good idea.

"You know Alex is not going to treat you right. He has never been anything other than a womanizer. When I told you back in the day that I kept seeing him with other women all the time, what did you tell me? 'Girl, it's nothing; he has a lot of women friends. He loves me.' Alex always knew that you would believe anything he said. Please, Peggy, don't put yourself through this again."

"I think he's telling the truth, he's changed."

"Open your eyes, Peggy. He is just feeling sorry for you and the kids right now. He is just saying the right things, but he doesn't mean it."

I told her I would think about it some more. Days went by, and I struggled with this. I decided to go for the kids.

"I guess I'll try again."

It was the month of April; we packed everything and moved. For the first few weeks everything was fine. All of us went to church together. He called his parents, telling them how happy he was to be back with his family. We were getting along pretty good when the phone began to ring; when I answered no one said anything.

I ask him what was going on. He said maybe they had the wrong number. Nothing else was said; late that night the phone rang, and he rushed to pick it up. He answered; I was right there on the other side of him. He wasn't doing much talking, more listening.

I said, "Who is that?"

He didn't answer. Again, "Who is that?"

Whoever was on the phone, I could hear the person talking real loud. I took the phone from him. I said, "Hello."

She said, "Hello. Who is this?"

So I replied, "No. Who is this?"

She said her name was Arlene, and she needed to know what I was doing over there. I said, "Oh, he didn't tell you?"

"Tell me what?"

"He's married. I'm his wife."

Well, he pulled the phone away from me and hung it up.

"So, Alex, who is Arlene?"

"Arlene is a friend of mine; I helped to move some furniture to her house."

Right away, he saw the look in my eyes. "No, not again," I thought. "I didn't let this man get me again." That night we went to bed with our backs facing each other.

Chapter Two

I can remember sleeping with my head under the covers. The next morning, the phone rang.

He said, "Don't answer it."

I asked him why.

He said, "Because I said so."

I said, "Because you said so?"

"This is my house, and I don't want any one answering this phone but me."

"Your house?"

"Yes, my house."

"Well, I'm your wife, and I live here too, so this is our house right?"

"Like I said, this is my house, my phone."

I went in the room and closed the door. Three days later the woman decided to pay him a visit to see for herself who I was. The car drove into the driveway; he had just got home from work. I was standing in the front door. I could see everything. Alex was already out of the car. He walked toward her car she got out. He was telling her to get back in the car. At that time, I came out of the house. I called Alex to see what was going on. He didn't answer. The woman got back in her car and drove off. I asked him what that was all about. He didn't answer.

"So you changed. What does that mean? Look, Alex, I didn't pick up me and the children and come all the way down here for this."

"Peggy, what are you talking about?"

"Please, Alex, I am not crazy. That was your woman. You didn't tell her that your family was coming to live with you, and that we are trying to start over."

"I did tell her."

"I heard everything she was saying, and she wanted me to."

"Peggy, I don't mess with that woman anymore; it's over."

"It's over for you, but she is not feeling the same way. I tell you what, Alex; you need to get your business together."

I got up and went to the store.

When I arrived back home, the kids came to get the bags out of the car. My oldest daughter told me that a woman just left, and that she and Daddy were yelling at each other.

"He told us to go in the house. When the lady left, he told us not to tell you. But, Momma, the lady was talking about you, telling Daddy that he told her that he didn't want you anymore."

At that point, I told my daughter that I had heard enough, and to go check on her sisters and brother.

I approached Alex; he knew what I was getting ready to say.

He told me that the lady was out of control. He was going to put a restraining order out on her. After that incident, Alex began to stay out all night long. I had nothing but flashbacks. I tried to stay with him as long as I could for the kids, but the disrespect was too obvious. Different women started to call the house at all times of the night. The very next summer I moved out; I found me a place in another part of town. Here I am again, but this time I filed for child support. I got my own job and got into a junior college. Boy, was he mad, but I didn't care. When he found out where we lived, he came over to the house raising hell. Telling me how I messed his life up.

"I never promised you a damn thing. You thought just because you had my kids and my mother loved you that it would change things between us. You knew I wasn't in love with you when we got married. When we were messing around I asked you not to get pregnant."

"What do you mean, you asked me not to get pregnant? It takes two to make a baby. Why didn't you wear a condom; ha, minister I don't want to have a baby."

By the time he got another word out the doorbell rang. I couldn't believe my eyes; it was Arlene, the woman he was sleeping with when I left him, and she had followed him to my house. It looked like she had something in her hand, and she did. It was a knife.

She began to yell, "You liar, you told me you were divorcing her."

Before he could say anything, she had stabbed him in the stomach twice—blood everywhere, kids crying and screaming. I told the children to get in the room and lock the door. I didn't know what was about to happen. My daughter called the police. It's me, Alex, and Arlene in the living room. Alex had fallen to his knees, holding his stomach; he was bleeding badly. I grabbed a vase off my table and yelled at her, "What have you done?" not knowing if I had to defend myself.

"Alex and I are not seeing each other, like it's any of your business anyway; he just finished telling me how much he hates me."

She looked at me and ran out the door.

The police got there just in time; she ran right into them. The kids crying, the ambulance got there, and blood was everywhere. I was trying to tell the police what happened and trying to keep the kids calm. It was terrible. They took her to jail, and I went to the hospital to see if he was okay. He was in critical condition. He didn't look so good. I got on the phone and called his parents to tell them what had happened. I went in to check on him, and he reached out his hand for me. I just looked at him. Slowly I went to his bedside. He was trying to tell me something. I leaned down to hear what he was trying to say. He asked me to tell his kids that he loved them, and that he was sorry for all the trouble he caused his kids, he said that I didn't deserve to raise them, he told me to take a good look at myself no one could ever love me. Your thin with barely no hair on your head. He was trying to say something else when I lean down and whisper in his ear, I feel sorry for you. He closed his eyes and died, never to hear his voice again. Finally it set in. He promised me nothing. Now I knew that Alex truly never loved me, and I would carry this bitter feeling in my heart for the rest of my life.

PICCOLA'S PLACE

When you went to this little town in Texas, you just had to stop by Piccola's Place; that's where they had food for the soul. Everything that came out of Piccola's kitchen was good. She prepared everything herself, and if it didn't taste right, she wasn't serving it. People go there sometimes just for conversation and laughter. Piccola's Place was a nice little restaurant, nice and clean; two of her daughters worked there with her. One early Sunday morning while getting the restaurant ready to open a young man walked in. He wasn't very clean, but he was really soft spoken. I asked him what I could get for him that morning.

He looked at me and said, "I only have one dollar. What could he get for a dollar?"

I told him, "I'm pretty sure I can find something."

I asked him if he drank coffee; he said yes.

I went into the kitchen and got him some grits and eggs, bacon, two biscuits, and a cup of coffee. When I came out with his food, he said, "Ms. Piccola, all this for a dollar?"

"Yes, but how do you know my name? I don't remember telling you my name."

"Ms. Piccola, people talk about you all the time, how nice you are to people and that you don't refuse anyone something to eat."

I asked him what his name was. He told me his name was Michael.

"Where do you live?"

He told me sometimes he goes to the shelter or to an abandoned house.

"Michael, why do you choose to live this way? You're no older than nineteen. What's going on with you? Where's your family?"

"I have been separated from my family since I was nine years old. My family disowned me because I was special."

"What do you mean, special?"

Michael got quiet; he refused to answer me.

"My grandmother who was taking care of me, she died four years ago; she was the only one who loved me. It was just her, and now I'm all alone. Growing up I had a lot of questions. At first I would try and ask my grandmother; after several attempts of getting no answers, I knew to keep my questions to myself. One day I overheard my grandmother talking to my mother on the phone. They were arguing about me. Grandmother was telling my mother how selfish she was; she told her that no matter what color I was, I was still her child. Come to find out that my skin was a little too dark and that I was drawing attention to the family. My father's family began to ask questions about how different I was from the other kids. My mother was lily-white, and so was my father. But somehow I came out dark. Looking at me you would think I was black or Hispanic. What do you think, Ms. Piccola?"

"Baby, I think you look like a handsome young man. That's all I see. A fine young man, to be exact." Michael found out later that his mother had an affair, and she was trying to keep it from his dad.

"But, Michael, how did you end up on the street? Didn't your grandmother own a home? Yes, ma'am, she does, but, Ms. Piccola, after I lost my grandmother I had no money to maintain the house, so it's just there. And I couldn't go home to my mother. I was teenage boy who she disowned."

He began to cry. I felt his pain.

"Okay, Michael, that's enough. You don't have to talk about it anymore if you don't want to."

"It's okay. I'm fine. I just wish my mother knew how much I miss her and my sisters."

I told Michael to come with me; I went to the back and told my girls that I would be right back. One of them asked where I was going with that strange man.

"Who is he?"

I introduced Michael to my daughters, and they knew how I was with people, so this wasn't strange to them at all. I took Michael to one of the local department stores and got him some new clothes, just something that would make him feel better. I brought him back to my house to take a bath; he asked me why I wasn't afraid of him, and why I was doing all this for him.

"You don't even know me."

Yes, I do. Your name is Michael. By the way, what is your last name?"

"Anderson is my last name."

I asked Michael if I had a reason to be afraid of him. He replied no. After he got clean, we went back to the restaurant. I gave him an apron and told him to clean this kitchen, and I needed all the dishes washed. A big smile came on his face.

"You mean I have a job?"

"I want you here every morning at eight o'clock sharp."

"Thank you, Ms. Piccola."

Michael washed all the dishes, and he was getting ready to leave. I called Michael into the dining area and asked him where he was sleeping that night. He looked at me and said, "Two blocks down in this empty house."

"No, you're not. You're getting your clothes and coming home with me."

Ms. Piccola had friends all over town. When they got home, she called one of her friends, David, over. He was a man who owned a group home for men. She asked him if Michael could stay there until he got on his feet. David said yes, under on one condition; he had to enroll in a community college. David had a talk with Michael.

"Ms. Piccola told me a little about you, and she believes in you. She says that there is so much more inside of you, and with a little help you can go far."

"Ms. Piccola says that about everybody."

"No, she doesn't; she calls a spade a spade. One thing you will learn about her is that she is a very good judge of character. They say she does see things."

That night Michael slept at Ms. Piccola's house; she wanted to have a good talk with Michael before he went to that halfway house. Michael was up and ready the next morning for work. He felt like a brand-new person. Ms. Piccola told him he had to go enroll in school first and then come to work. That's exactly what he did. When he got back to Piccola's Place, everyone was so amazed at how clean he was and how different he looked. Piccola's daughter asked him what is his major in college. He told them biology.

"Why biology?"

"Oh, I was thinking about one day going to medical school."

Both of them looked at each other. No one knew that Michael was a straight-A student and one of the top in his class. But Ms. Piccola saw something in his eyes.

Michael worked for Ms. Piccola for two years before he took a job at the local hospital, as a student worker, and he had transferred to a four-year college, Texas A&M University. Ms. Piccola was getting a report on Michael's grades, and he had moved out of the halfway house back into his grandmother's house. Michael was repairing his grandmother's house, restoring all the wood that had rotted. He promised Ms. Piccola that he wouldn't quit. Time passed, and Michael had started his clinical, getting ready to become a doctor. Graduation time was coming, and Michael had only four invitations to pass out—Ms. Piccola and her two daughters and Mr. David from the halfway house where he had lived. Graduation was in three weeks, and he was getting ready, but I noticed this emptiness about him. I asked Michael if anything was wrong, and he said no. I knew something was wrong with my Michael. I got on the phone, called one of my old friends, and asked her if she could do me a big favor. I asked her to find Michael's parents. I knew his mother's name was Gloria Anderson. My friend told me to let her see what she could do. Two weeks passed, and she called and said she found Michael's mother. But there was some bad news; his father had passed. Piccola took all the information down and told Michael that she needed to talk to him. He told her he would be there by one o'clock. Michael got there, and Jenny and Missy, Piccola's two daughters, were there. Michael asked why everybody was looking so serious. Piccola said she had some good news and some bad news to tell him. The girls had cooked a big dinner. They told Michael how proud they were of him.

"I knew you could do it."

Michael asked, "What is the news?"

Piccola told him that she had found his family.

He said, "My family? What family? Ms. Piccola, you know I don't have a family"

"I found your mother and father."

Michael got quiet for a while. We just waited for him to say something.

He said, "Why? They don't love me; they hate me. I don't want to see them."

"Michael, your father is dead; he died of lung cancer last year.

"He wasn't my father; he never came to get me. He knew where I was. He didn't even ask questions about why she gave me, his only son and his first child, to my grandmother.

Michael began to cry.

"I wish my grandmother could see me now."

I got up, went to the other side of the table, wrapped my arms around him, and told him, "Your grandmother knows, and she is very proud of you. Michael it's all right to be angry; it's all right."

After Michael got it all out, I told him that he needed to talk to his mother.

"What if she doesn't want to talk to me?"

"Well, then it's all on her."

The next week Michael was graduating, with honors. It weighed heavily on his mind what he would say to his mother after all that time. Michael decided to call her. He called the number Ms. Piccola gave him, and a young woman answered the phone. She asked him who was calling; he told her his name.

She said, "No, this can't be. My brother name is Michael, and he is dead."

At that point, he asked to speak to her mother.

The young women said, "No. Stop playing games on this phone," and she hung up. The next time he called his mother answered the phone.

"Who is this?"

"Michael."

She heard his voice, and she knew that it was him. She didn't say anything for a minute.

He said, "Mother, are you there?"

"Yes."

"I need to talk to you. I'm not looking for anything; I just need to talk to you."

She agreed and gave him the address. He told her he was on his way over; she lived about forty-five minutes away. When Michael got there, his two sisters were standing in the door. He got out of the car, and they ran over to greet him. They took him in the house, and his mother was sitting in the chair facing the window; she was so ashamed to look him in the face. She turned to look at him and began crying; he held her and told her that he never forgot about them and that he always kept a picture of them in his mind. After his mother stopped crying, she asked her daughters to leave the room. What Michael's mom didn't know was that he was just as afraid as she was. Michael asked her why she didn't love him, and why he wasn't good enough to be a part of that family. How could she give him away? She told him that she didn't know what to do; she was young, with a wealthy man, and she had to make a decision. She knew that he wasn't for her husband; it was either give him up or tell her husband the truth.

Michael told her, "So, Mother, that's the choice you made. What about owning up to what you did, being a woman about it? Telling Daddy what you did and letting the chips fall where they may. Who knows, Mother, he might have kept your secret. Maybe he would have loved me anyway, but you made that choice for him. Now you will never know; he is dead."

Michael turned and began to walk away.

"You know what, Mother, it doesn't even matter. What you need to know is, I'm a good person, a good man, and I work hard. I don't steal, and I don't carry a gun. I am graduating from the Texas A&M University next week, and leaving for medical school in August. I just had to hear for myself why I wasn't good enough. Granny did what she could for me, but you never once sent her any money to help. You didn't even come to her funeral. Why, mother? Were you afraid you were going to have to see me?"

I got up, and on the way out my two sisters were crying and saying they were sorry because they didn't ask questions.

"Momma told us you were dead; we were eight and six years old. Please don't leave us."

I kissed both of them on the forehead and told them I loved them and slipped them my telephone number and address to my grandmother's house. I returned home, and Ms. Piccola called me. She wanted me to come over; she had cooked. I knew what she wanted; she wanted to know what happened at my mom's house. When I got there she gave me a big kiss and held me real tight. Then she asked me if I was all right.

"Yes."

"What happened?"

"Well, my mother told me what I already knew. She just confirmed it for me. She told me the sad story about being afraid of losing her rich husband, who I knew as Daddy. How could she do something like that, Ms. Piccola? I couldn't even yell and tell her how lonely I was and how she hurt me. I couldn't say any of the things I really wanted to say, just looking at her telling me what she thought she had to do. I didn't want to be there anymore."

Two days later Michael graduated, and he went on to medical school. He tried to keep in contact with his sisters. They were calling him every chance they got. Before Michael knew it, his sisters both began to sneak off to visit him. They told him that his mother wasn't doing well. I discussed how I was feeling with Ms. Piccola. I told her that I didn't really know how I felt about my mother.

"I'm not feeling anything right now. I don't feel like going to see about her."

Ms. Piccola sat me down and told me about forgiveness. She told me the story about Jesus. She asked me if I knew that Jesus died for the very men who hung him on the cross, for the ones who stabbed him in his side, and for the men who beat him. She told me that I had no choice but to forgive her.

"I know you don't understand how, but in time you will."

What Ms. Piccola told me stayed on my mind. That night I had a dream; this dream was as real as it gets. I saw my mother on a road looking for something or someone. I followed her in this dream, trying to catch up with her, but I never did. I could hear my mother crying, yelling, "Please. I am so sorry; forgive me." That's all I could hear her saying.

And then Ms. Piccola told me that my mother was going through her own battle, and she was suffering deep inside.

"She wants to tell you how sorry she is, but her pride and shame won't let her. She knows that you have made it without any help or accommodations from her, and you are the man you knew as your father. Her hurt runs deeper than anything you can ever impose on her. I know your grandmother is looking down at her grandson proudly, knowing she raised such a fine man. Michael, I know you're been through a lot, but you made it."

"Don't forget about you, Ms. Piccola. I don't know where I would be if you weren't in my life. You gave me a job, a place to stay, and included me in your family; I will always love you for that. Who would have thought, looking back at my life a couple of years ago. Ms. Piccola, I remember how I was and how I was living. You took me in with no questions asked. I never met anyone like you before; I was told once that there are angels walking among us. I believe it now, and you have been truly a blessing.

"Remember what I told you. It's never over until God says so. Now go and see your mother, and let her say what she's been longing to tell you."

"I am afraid to see her again."

"Why? There needs to be some kind of closure."

I reached for the phone and called his mom. When she heard his voice she told him that she was just thinking about him; she didn't think she would ever hear his voice again. His mother told him that his sisters told her about Ms. Piccola and her daughters, and how nice they were to him. He asked her if he could come to see her.

"Please, Michael, I would love to see you."

Michael arrived at his mother's house, and she was alone; his sisters were gone. She gave him a big hug and asked him to sit down. She started by telling him that she had never stopped thinking about him and that his sisters would always ask questions about where he was.

"I told them that you had taken sick and died. I am so sorry. I let my fear and selfishness control me making the right decision. There was only one thing I could have done, and that was telling your father the truth about what I had done. Instead, I hid it from him. Mainly everything I did was from fear. You have to believe me; I had so much fear of losing your father and giving up this lifestyle. Michael, one thing I came to realize, and that is your father already knew. Baby, if I could take it all back I would, but you can believe that I am sorry, and if you can't forgive me I understand."

I looked at my mother and said, "All is forgiven."

I told her I had lived on the streets.

"I was lost with no hope, trying to understand what I had done to make you give me away, not being able to call you or my sisters. Granny makes up stories to cover up the fact that you just didn't care. Granny was everything to me; she was all I had. Mother, I sat here and listened to every word you said, and yet I still feel empty. What did you tell him? Did my father ever ask about me? He didn't care what happened to his own son. I guess you're right; he did know. My sisters thought I was dead. I guess all there is left for you to say is you are sorry. Mother, we lost a lot of time. I want my sisters to know their big brother. I want to always be there for them, and, Mother, I hope your life has given you all the happiness you were hoping for."

That day I left my mother's house, never to return.

ESCORT ME

Chapter One

In today's society, there are so many hypocrites. Being the people to whom the public looks for objective information, the research journalists and academic scholars seem to distort the realities of the issue. It is difficult to trust studies or statistics, many of which contradict each other, when women are abducted or sold for sexual purposes. Why can't I have the right to sell myself? Men and women in high positions pretend they don't call for my services. This is one of the oldest professions in the world. Some say escort services don't sell sex. Being in the escort business you learn one thing; there are so many ways to escort these men and women. I don't know what planet you've been living on, but the love of power, money, and sex makes the world go around. Prostitution, denied and hidden, the lust, the corruption, and the wealth behind what we refer to as call girls.

Pretend if you must, but don't stop calling. As a young teenager, I had thoughts of running my own escort service. I knew several young ladies that would be interested in something like that. In my senior year, I had my plan together and down on paper. After graduation, I moved to New York City. There I met and got close to some of what we call high-class people. I had my business cards made and passed them out to a few people, not knowing who I could trust yet, and testing the water myself to see exactly how I wanted my operation to run. I worked alone for about three months. Business was good. I knew it was time for me to expand. I had one client who was very well-known and who had power in big places. If I may add, he was more than just a client; in a way he was a backdoor business partner. Most of his associates became my customers. I called a couple of my girlfriends, told them a little bit about it and the money that could be made, and asked if they would consider flying down to New York to meet with me. Four of them came down together. I told them how much money they would make and what they were expected to do. Out of the four of them, three decided to join. One wanted more from me than I was willing to give. I had a plan, and I was sticking to it. I told those who had decided to join to go back home and gather their personal things, and that I would expect them to return the next month. The girls returned, and business was booming. My clients were from all parts of the world; it was growing fast. I had to recruit more girls. Being in this business, I knew I had to be careful. I created applications with terms and agreements; there were no medical benefits, so they had to get their own. One of my agreements was no dating clients. One of the girls I was real close to, Cindy, I promoted to be my assistant; she was real sharp and had business experience that would help me out a lot. She also had training in finance.

I had a nice office space, clerical staff, and payroll staff; it was on. I ran my escort service very professionally. My clients, I would say, were well-to-do—lawyers, judges, senators, and governors. They would refer their friends, that way there were no outsiders. At the end of the year, one of the girls decided to break her contract. She had an affair with one of the clients; she just knew they were in love, and he was going to leave his wife. Okay, here goes the first problem for my business. I called her into my office to talk with her about the situation, and she gave me attitude. I told her, "Listen, when I asked you to be a part of this business, I told you what I expected from you, and you signed a contract. I am not only trying to protect my business, I am protecting my girls."

"Protecting me? How are you protecting me?"

"This is an escort service; we serve men. Do you really think that he wants to take you home and marry you? The men that come here are only looking for one thing, and one thing only. You're being his escort for whatever length of time he pays for. That's all; that's it. How could you allow yourself to get caught up in your work?"

She said she didn't mean to.

"This particular client would start taking me with him to dinner parties, and the conversation was always personal. I would ask him to talk about something else instead of his wife, but I would listen to him anyway. Half of the time, all he wanted to do was talk. He even cried sometimes. He would call me all times of the night."

"What do you mean, call you? That's not how I run my service; anyone who needs an escort can contact my office. So you're telling me that he has your personal number?"

It got quiet for a minute.

"So, let's talk. Are you running your own business on the side?"

"No, it's not like that."

"Well, what's going on?"

"Listening to his sad story, I began to feel for him."

"Listen, Pam, when you joined in, you signed a written agreement that states that personnel are not to date customers.

"I know, Cheryl, but it just happened."

"Well, Pam, you know you broke the contract."

"Yes, I know."

"I am going to have to let you go. I have ten girls to monitor, and I talk to you girls all the time. When were you going to tell me about this? I am sorry, Pam."

"I'm sorry too."

I hated to let Pam go, but I had to; the other girls knew about the affair, but no one told me. The following day, I called a staff meeting. Everyone was sitting at the table looking all around; no one could really look me in the face. They began talking about the contract they signed. I pulled it out and went over it again. I asked if they were tired of following the rules.

"If so, let me know, and you can be dismissed."

I asked Cindy if she knew anything about this. She told me no; she hadn't a clue. I reminded her how much I trusted her. She assured me that she had my back.

Chapter Two

The next couple of months went fine; there was news in the grapevine that one of the girls that used to work for me was now running her own escort service. Okay, I knew she didn't know enough to pull it off; she had help from someone. I didn't panic. I made a couple of calls and found out where her office was. I made it my business to pay her a visit. Little did I know that her business partner was one of my old clients—the man she was in love with. When I came into her office, she was surprised to see me. I could tell she was just getting it together. Boxes were everywhere; it was just her. She didn't have a staff yet, it was obvious.

"Is this what you wanted?"

"I know you don't think you're the only one who could pull something off like this."

"No. If this was something you wanted to do, why didn't you just say so? I didn't come to start a fight; I just wanted to see for myself if what I heard was true. You know, one thing you learn in this business, all is fair in the game. Let's see how much you have. I started my business solo, with my own money. I am my own boss. Who's yours? See you on the way down."

Cindy was yelling, "You're not the only one who can do it."

I turned to Cindy and said, "By the way, are you married yet?"

She yelled for me to get out.

After that she was in competition with me. I was ready. Cindy thought that she was going to steal my clients, but little did she know that most of the clients I had were very close friends. They were my first clients, who introduced my service to my newer clients, which already gave me a sense of security. And what I didn't expose to her was that the man she thinks she is in love with is my ex-lover. I'm sure he hasn't told her either, because she would have said something. I will just wait and see how long he will keep this secret from her. I let Cindy go for it; meanwhile, behind the scenes, I was showing her man just enough attention to start his curiosity. Phone calls from "her" Danny began to come in at my office. He would leave me messages; some I would return, and some I wouldn't. I was pulling him in little by little. I kept an eye on Cindy to see how her business was going. The word was she was not making enough. She was spending more than she was making, and the love of her life was nowhere to be found, unless he wanted to be. He was bringing me new clients, trying to impress me, but I knew how to play the game. I kept his nose open until I saw her on the way down, like I told her. When she found out that Danny and I used to see each other, she wanted to kill me. I told Cindy if she wasn't so busy trying to be sneaky and had talked to me, since she said she was in love, I could have told her that Danny and I used to date. But she called herself getting over. And as for Danny, I didn't want him either; it was all part of the game. One thing I did learn in the game is that business is business. One of the things Danny and I both understood is that nothing gets in the way of the money. Danny was part of my networking, something she hadn't learned yet. My business continued to grow, and I became the richest madam of New York, known all around the world even today.

BITTER WOMEN

What goes on in most marriages? Do we make more out of marriage than it needs to be? Or maybe we don't make enough out of it. Does marriage make a person complete? What if you never marry? Then what? Growing up, we are taught that marriage is one of the most sacred things two people will encounter in their lives. Today people fall in lust or in need but not in love. What happened to having morals and values? The values of love are just respecting people. For those who read this story and feel offended, all I can say is if the shoe fits, wear it. I'm sitting here in my office thinking about all of the conversations I've had with some married women, or something I've heard from friends.

Talking to husbands about their wives, just listening to them, makes me sick half of the time, bragging, saying, girl, I'm not doing this; I'm not doing that; if he wants all that he better go somewhere else. They have so many limitations, you won't even believe, when it comes to having sex. Oh, I forgot to mention the limitation comes after marriage. They turn their nose up to single women as if we are beneath them. Do they really think that they are better? I don't think so. You've probably heard the saying, you make your husband think that he's running the show, but in reality you are. I have asked myself how I can give my opinion without the hater coming out thinking, "Oh, she just another bitter woman." No, bitter I'm not, just tired of married women judging everybody else but themselves. Hiding behind her husband, pretending to be a traditional family, but for the people out there who know his wife in ways he doesn't, she's a trick.

"Bitter Women"

Married women are just as tricky as any other woman, and maybe even more so. Some talk to their husband as if they have tails. Some treat them like kids. For the man that holds his own, good for you. Some women think because they can go around saying my husband this, my husband that, gives them a sense of pride and respect that they didn't feel before they were married. A lot of wealthy men married women with the promise of good finances, in one way or another, or so they think. She has him blind by the hype. Some marry trophy wives because they are pretty; they love to have them on their arms. Some marry because she is pregnant; some marry whores and try to turn them into housewives, and some are insecure and needy. But how many women marry their husbands because they truly loved them? They listen to others: Oh, don't worry, you'll fall in love with him; he's a good man; or, girl, you better marry that man, he has a good job, not knowing about the other things that man has, like wife beating or womanizing. I know, I could go on and on.

"Bitter Women"

Married women like to have their cake and eat it too. Some women are so afraid of being along; some think after a certain age you are considered an old maid. Some women are lazy and don't want to work, so they marry for stability, or to help them raise their children from other relationships or marriages. What happened to marrying for love? You know what they say: what's love got to do with it? We have the women that the husband is no good in bed, but he makes a great deal of money.

"I guess that's okay. I'll just get a lover on the side."

Then there's the husband with no money that makes you feel like you're on cloud nine in bed.

"I guess that's okay. I'll just get a sugar daddy." Oh, I'm sorry, wives, if I am giving out your secrets, but enough is enough already.

"Bitter Women"

Many married women are better at role playing than some of the actresses we see on television. A lot of them are cheaters, but he thinks he is the only one. Most women marry men they can control. The man doesn't see it until it's too late and too far into the marriage with children. Now they are married, lonely, and hungry for love. She thinks that she has it all wrapped up. But little does she know there are women on the outside looking in, watching patiently, and waiting for the opportunity to step right in, because there is always one woman who thinks she can do better than the next. Now, what do we have here? The single woman down the street or women on the job or maybe even the women at the neighborhood store; we can go further than that, how about the married woman whose husband doesn't show her any attention. The man doesn't realize how lonely he really is until another women starts to show him a little attention. No excuses; it doesn't make it right, but this is how things happen the majority of the time.

"Bitter women"

Now we have problems. The wife is in love again. Yeah, right. She is not in love and never was; she's just watching her bank. His money is her money. Now one of several things could happen: the husband could fall in love with the other woman and have kids outside of the marriage, or this can become a new-found habit of sleeping around, or the wife just may wake up and smell the coffee. I know you've heard of the clean-up woman. She gets all the love you women leave behind and more. She gets more because her t's are crossed and her i's are dotted. It's on in the wife's world. Her focus will change; her husband will become her main concern again. His wants and needs will be important to her again. She will be getting ready to get a dose of her own medicine.

Some married women may come out of it standing, but most don't. It's harder when the shoe is on the other foot. Forgetting about the past year, him trying to reach her, having sex once a month or not at all, or her pulling away from him and leaving him in a state of confusion, thinking and trying to do what he can to get closer to her.

Trying to hold your marriage together alone is a no-win situation.

"Bitter Women"

Have you ever known anyone in love with his or her spouse, and one of them is trying and the other just doesn't care? So they pretend. So, what happens when there is this void? They look for attention elsewhere, some willingly, and some don't even realize how empty and lonely they really are. If you pay attention to some of the married men in the workplace, or someone you may even know, a lot are very unhappy. They are horny all the time. What about the husband that sleeps in a separate room? Check this out. Some may even live in different homes. Some men have to make an appointment to have sex with their wife. What you think about that? Some are raising kids that are not even biologically theirs, and the husband knows it in his heart but is too afraid to find out because if he does, that will confirm the feeling that he was fighting deep inside. For the women out there who are cheating with married men just to get their bills paid, get a Job!

"Bitter Women"

In this world today there many forms of marriage arrangements that take away from the true meaning of marriage. What happened to the good old days when you date, fell in love, got married and had children or not. People used to truly love their mates, respected each other, and have morals and values. Some women feel like all men cheat; sometimes that's just an excuse so she can feel right about what she's doing—be it cheating or disrespecting him in front of family and friends. I have seen this happen where the wife belittles her husband in front of company, and he walks around with his head down for the rest of the evening. Today's women have turned the table on who wears the pants. Yeah, right, what does wearing the pants mean? The wife makes all the decisions. That's just an old saying that really means nothing. Marriage is all about respecting and loving each other, having values and morals, and believing in one another. Having each other's back. I know you're reading this and saying, "What is her problem?" My problem is that we as women need to respect ourselves and other women, and just maybe if we did, a cheating man wouldn't have the opportunity to cheat.

"Bitter Women"

It seemed pretty amazing that most married women control their husbands with sex. Oh, yeah, before they married the man, they did all the things it took to get to him and more. He couldn't breathe without ass everywhere, or just the small things, such as having dinner together or saying I love you from time to time. And as single women we often wonder while dating, why men act and say things like, "I'm just waiting for that other side to come out." We know that all women aren't bad, just as all men don't cheat. This story is for the woman that reads this and can identify herself in this to take a long look at self and say that they deserve more than a one-night stand or years of a married man promising and lying that he will leave his wife because of all the heartaches she brings. But what you don't realize is that by your being there for him, getting him ready for you to release him from all his stress and madness, you are left in the cold, with no one to ease your pain. I guess you're satisfied with him just being there. Being there doing what? Nothing, nothing but getting himself ready to go back home to his wife, where he can get up in the morning to go to work and take care of that wife who "treats him like dirt."

"Bitter Women"

Now everything is about him, leaving you empty and your desires unmet. Yeah, you go around thinking and telling your girlfriends and everybody else that you don't want to be married, and you're in control. But are you really? Be true to yourself. How does it feel when he goes home to his wife, and you just told him you love him, and you're in love with him? Doing the things that his wife doesn't do, but yet he goes home. Don't think that for once I'm standing up for men who cheat. Not at all. This is to open the eyes of those who are blinded by deception, or for women who have no self-esteem.

Some married women blame everyone else for their husband's affairs instead of facing the facts. It takes two; the husband can always say no, I'm married. What about addressing the problem when it occurs, and stop thinking it will fix itself. Either both of you are running from each other and pretending that there is no problem, or one is trying and the other has the "whatever" attitude. There are so many lost marriages; some marry the man or woman to keep him or her from someone else. Oh, boy, I just stepped on somebody's toes. Some married women feed on getting away with having affairs.

"Bitter Women"

Most married women consider themselves better than single women because they get to say "my husband." Some married women envy single women because they can't move around and do what they want without hiding. They want people to think that everything is all good. But in reality they have a man for every occasion. Well, can you say that the man you call your husband loves you, and you feel it in your heart? That's what I thought. I didn't think so. Maybe you can say he loves you because he married you. Is that the case? For the woman who has a job or career, if you're not kissing his butt or boosting his ego, you guys are yelling at each other all the time. What a life. If this life is good for you, then this means nothing to you. But for the women out there who can feel what I'm saying, don't get offended. Get mad at what's been going on in your life, and say no more.

"Bitter Women"

Now, don't get me wrong. There are people in this world who have been blessed to have been loved and have loved in return for better or for worse, through thick and thin, until death do they part. Oh, but not many. I say to all people, men or women, live each day with an open mind and an open heart; listen to that voice inside of you. Remember what's right and what's wrong. Learn what makes you happy. Time goes on; when you're dead, you're done. The trouble with some people is that they are so afraid of being themselves and are afraid of what people might say or think about them. But the truth of the matter is your friends and families don't have a heaven or hell to put you in after this life. Stop cheating yourself out of happiness, peace, joy, and hope.

"Bitter Women"

I'm tired of married women judging everybody else but themselves. Stop hiding and get real. Own up to what part you play with these cheating husbands of yours. Quit making them feel like they're all that, when in fact they're not. Tell them the truth. If he is not good in bed, tell him, show him, and learn together. If he says something you don't like, tell him. What's the most that can happen? He's going to leave you? I don't think so, but if he does, you didn't need him anyway. Ladies, take the time to know your man. Pay attention, and listen. Hear with your heart, not just with your ears. Because you just might miss something. It is so easy to miss something that you really need to hear. You need to hear it because your spouse wants and need you to understand, and agree or disagree. And I guarantee you things will click. If he is a cheater, he was a cheater before you married him. Stop marrying men and trying to change them after you are married. Either you love him for who he is and how he is, or you don't. But what you can't do is fake the funk.

Bitter woman I'm not!

SHE'S ALL I'VE GOT

Chapter One

Today is a good day for working out. I got up this morning and didn't have to go to work. I was thinking about how to begin my day, when the phone rang. It was Venson; he asked if he could come over. I told him that I was going for a walk. He asked if he could join me. I said no, but maybe next time. Venson is the kind of guy that's real nice looking, and the women are always all over him. We went together to work functions I had to attend or he had to attend. We did practically everything together, but there was only one problem. He has never asked me to be his woman. Why? Why should he? I don't even know if he feels the same way I do. Venson is my lover; I can't really call him my man yet. I began to think about what if I told him that I wanted more and that I wanted us to make a commitment to each other. The next day, I did. After I asked him about being committed to each other, he didn't visit much. I would hear from him from time to time. Monday morning I got up and turned on the TV; there was a big accident on the freeway. Several cars were involved—some turned over, some smashed. Fire trucks and a helicopter were on the scene. One of the cars looked just like Venson's car, and it was. I immediately called his cell phone, but there was no answer. I called one of his friends that I knew, and there was no answer. I called every hospital to find him, and I did. He was in critical condition; when I arrived at the hospital he had already passed.

Two months passed, and my life felt at a standstill. I began to call some of my friends to catch up on old times. No one was available to talk, so I sat down and begin to write, just writing the things I felt deep inside of me. While writing, I realized that I have been trying to please everybody but me. That's when I met Joe; he was tall, dark, and handsome. Our eyes met at the same time. He came over to the table where I was seated and introduced himself. At that time, I had finished eating and was drinking a martini; he had a drink in his hand, and I asked if he wanted to sit down. He did. We talked and laughed, exchanged phone numbers, and said good night. Well, two nights later he called and asked me out, and I said yes, of course. He took me to the Kodak Theater to see the O'Jays concert; we really had a good time. After that date, we began to see each other regularly. At first I thought this is too good to be true. He always had time for me, and we would go places together. On our first date, we sat down and talked about how we how felt about certain things, and what we looked for in a relationship. Honesty was the main concern for both of us. He told me that he had been married once, and had been in and out of relationships for about four years, and he had stopped looking. I told him that I never really looked for a man; they always showed up. I told him that I also was married once, was divorced and had a couple of friends, but nothing serious.

Well, the next day Joe asked me to go to Lake Charles, Louisiana, for the weekend. I told him that I had other plans. He said he was not trying to get in my business, what kind of plans? I looked at him and said, "One of my friends called last night to invite me to a party."

"Well, are you going?"

"Yes."

"How about you calling that friend back and saying you're sorry, but you forgot that you were going to be out of town this weekend. I knew how important spending this weekend was to him. Okay, I called my friend back. I told Joe that I would talk to him later; I had to pack. Joe called me with his plans. I got excited, and I drove to his house and left my car there for the weekend. On the way we were listening to all his old CDs, Motown favorites. The sky was cloudy. Looks like rain. By the time we got to Lake Charles, it began to rain; there was Lake Charles beach. Joe jumped out of the car. I got out behind him.

"What are you doing? It's raining?"

We walked on Lake Charles beach, dancing in the rain. Joe started singing; we were soaking wet.

"Joe, are you crazy? We both are going to get sick."

"Don't say that. Just enjoy yourself."

I ran to the car. He came to the car.

"Joe, get in the car, before you get sick, okay."

He got in and drove to the hotel; we took a hot shower and got ready for dinner, and then had a couple of martinis before dinner. Everything was nice. Off the main lobby there was this huge patio; you could see the sunset. We began to look each other in the eyes. Okay, I am feeling this. He reached over and kissed me real soft, again and again. He picked me up and took me inside. He tripped over something and fell down with me; we laughed and kissed and made mad love right there on the floor. Now we were worrying if anybody had seen us. We got up. I'm all wet between the legs—dress wet. He has spots on his pants. We walked off the patio like nothing happened. Everything was beautiful; I could feel my heart opening up. Oh, my god, what's going on? Not knowing how to enjoy the moment. From out of nowhere, I began to say ugly things to him. It was like another person trying to show herself. I began to pull back; I felt scared inside. Joe looked at me and grabbed my hand.

"What's wrong? Did I say something?"

This was the first time Joe had seen me like this.

"I'm okay. Just leave me alone."

That left Joe puzzled, not knowing what to do. He went into the other room; my head was hurting real bad. I hadn't had this kind of headache for about a year. For a long time, I told myself when it comes to being in a relationship I try not to get serious because with my condition, relationships don't last. I try to enjoy what I can and keep my feelings out of it. But this was different. I felt like we had known each other for a long time.

Right then I was fighting myself, thinking, "should I go for it or step back?" He keeps telling me that he notices this outer space look, as if my mind was always somewhere else, trying to figure something out, and that I'm never relaxed. The first time he saw me with my guards down was the weekend we were in Lake Charles. Trying to keep Melissa away from him was beginning to cause problems. I didn't want to run him away, or him to think I am crazy. I hoped that it hadn't gotten that bad. So for months we dated, and I introduced him to my family and friends. I met his mother, his sister Carol, and his two brothers, Pete and Earl. He seemed to come from a well-grounded family. I was trying to hide the fact that I hadn't told Joe everything about me. It's enough, he says. Sometimes I act peculiar. Joe would sometimes ask me if I was feeling okay.

"Why?" I would ask.

"Because you are acting strange."

"Strange, like what?"

"Your voice doesn't always sound the same."

It was my chance to tell him the truth, but I was afraid. Early that Sunday morning, I called him to ask if he was coming to church with me, and there was no answer. I waited as long as I could, and then I went on to church. After church, I called Joe to tell him that I was on my way over, but he didn't answer. So I went over anyway. His car was outside of the garage, and that was odd because he always parked inside the garage. Well, I got out and went to the door, and I could hear the TV on, but no one answered the door. I looked in the window on the garage door; parked inside was a red car. Oh, boy, my heart is beating fast. I got on my cell phone and called his house phone. No answer. And then I called his cell phone. No answer. Later on that night Joe called and said that he was sorry he missed my call, but he was at a Big Brothers meeting with his sister's son.

I said, "Is that right? Did you ride with your sister?"

"Yes, I did," he replied.

"I came over to your house after church, and your car was in the driveway. Joe, whose red car was that in your garage? Your sister's car is blue."

He replied, "What red car? There was never a red car in my garage."

With that answer, I didn't say another word. I told him that I would talk to him later. How do I handle this? I didn't speak to Joe for about a week or so. I would wait late and drive by Joe's house to see if there was anyone there. The first two nights he was home alone. I felt bad. Melissa was still trying her best to show herself; she wants to handle this for me. I kept telling her no, go away. Between her and Donna, I don't know which one is the worst. The next week when I did talk to him, the conversation was short and dry. His attitude had changed. I asked, "What's up? You sound different."

And he said, "I was thinking about when you said you saw a red car in my garage? What kind of person looks in other person's windows?"

I said, "What? First of all, I called your house, and cell phone, and you didn't pick up the phone. If I didn't answer that means I wasn't home. I thought maybe you couldn't get to the phone. So I came over. Am I your girl?"

"Yes, you are."

"Okay, when you didn't answer the phone, I decided to check on you. When I got to your house, your car was in the driveway. I knocked on the door. No answer. I heard the TV on, and that's when I looked into the garage window and saw the red car."

Before I could stop her, Melissa lashed out, "Who do you think you are? Playing games already; I never liked you in the first place."

Joe didn't know what was going on. Looking at me, he said, "Linda, stop yelling at me."

"Linda, my name isn't Linda."

"What do you mean, your name is not Linda?"

"Don't act like you never saw me before. I saw the way you were looking at me."

"What are you talking about?"

"You always wanted me from the first time you met Linda."

"All right, what is going on?"

Linda passed out on the floor. When she came to, Joe had called her sister. Joe had told her sister that Linda had passed out and he didn't know what was going on with her; she didn't want to go to the doctor. She was acting strange. Darlene told Joe that he needed to talk to Linda. It wasn't her place to tell him about Linda's illness. Joe was puzzled; he didn't have a clue. Linda was crying and upset; she didn't know how to tell Joe about her illness. Instead, she started an argument with Joe. I didn't forget what he said when we were talking about me coming over to your house.

"What do you mean, what kind of person looks into a garage window? You said there was no red car in your garage, so I guess I was seeing things. Or are you calling me a liar?"

"No I did not say that."

Joe says, "Is there something I need to know?"

"What do you mean, 'Is there something I need to know?'"

This was the first time I had heard Joe talk like this. You could hear the anger in his voice.

"Joe, you sound upset."

He replied, "No, not upset. I feel violated."

"Well, I'm sorry you feel that way. When I came to your house, I had no bad intentions. Look, Joe, when you decide to tell me what's going on, call me. Because whatever is going on, you feel you have to lie about it. I know one thing. I am not blind, and I know what I saw."

All the drama with Joe took his attention from me telling him about my illness. I broke it off with Joe and told him that we should just be friends. Joe told me that he was getting ready to take a trip to Jersey on business. While Joe was in Jersey, I drove by his house, and in the driveway was that same red car. This time as I was driving by, the door opened. Joe and this Hispanic female and little kid came running out; at that time Joe was looking my way, and he saw me; I kept on driving. The next day Joe called me.

"To whom do I owe this pleasure?"

He said, "I just thought I would call to see how you were doing."

"Is that so? How was Jersey?"

He replied, "The meeting went fine."

I said, "You need to stop already—lie, lie, and lie, one after another. You seen me driving by your house last night; you looked dead in my face."

"I got in town about midnight."

"I guess I'm still seeing things, because I saw you and a Hispanic female and the kids going to your car in front of your house about eight last night. I know it was you."

He said he didn't want to talk about it anymore.

"Whatever, Joe!"

Come to find out that the woman I saw him with was his wife of ten years, and she had been away for four months, taking care of her mother. Now, I was thinking, how could that be? I met your mother, your sister, and your brother."

Then I got upset because Joe told me I reminded him of his mother. No, I don't because there is no way anyone in my family would introduce me to another man, knowing that I am married.

"My mother just wants me to be happy, is that right? Does being happy mean seeing other women when your wife is away?"

Melissa shows up.

"You're just like the rest of them, pretending you're different. I hate all of you."

Melissa walks up to Joe and begins to fight him; he grabs her hands.

"Stop, Linda, before you hurt yourself."

"I told you, my name is not Linda."

By that time, Joe could not calm Linda down; all the ladies had showed themselves, Joe holding this person down. He didn't know what to do. She passed out just like before. He didn't call her sister this time. Joe waited for her to wake up.

When she came to, Joe asked, "What's wrong with you. I can't believe what just happened before my very eyes. I saw you, I mean Melissa, no Donna, and Kathy. You were trying to kill me."

What's wrong with you are you sick?

"It really doesn't make a difference what's wrong with me. Yes, I have multiple personality disorders. I wasn't ready to tell you yet, and I am glad I didn't. You were never serious about me anyway. I know one thing, sick are not, your mother needs to tell you what you're doing is wrong."

After that incident, I didn't hear from Joe anymore. Linda was gone; the ladies had taken over. Melissa finally got what she wanted, to take total control of Linda's life. Linda lost in her own head. The friends she had backed away from her, they found her to be straight. Melissa called her sister, Arlene, and told her that she was thinking about moving to New York. Arlene rushed over to Linda's house. She heard the difference in her voice; she thought she heard Donna. She and Donna had a run-in before. When she got there, Melissa opened the door for her. Arlene asked her if she was she okay, and asked why she was moving away. Right off, Melissa yelled, "Why does it always have to be something wrong with me? Calm down, Linda. Linda, there you go. My name is Melissa. I wish everyone would stop calling me Linda; she's such a bore.

I'm sorry, Melissa, my mistake. Why do you want to move?"

"I'm tired of this small town; everyone knows each other. I'm moving forward with my life. I've been held down too long."

Arlene knew she had to handle this with care. She asked Melissa if she had found a job in New York. Did she have a place to stay?

Melissa began to panic. "Stop asking me all these questions. None of your business. I am moving to New York, and that's all you need to know."

Arlene sat down. "Are you hungry?"

Melissa said yes. They went into the kitchen to see what they could come up with. They decided to make a salad.

Melissa felt like dancing. Arlene was trying to be careful of what she said. She told Melissa it was too late to go dancing that night.

"This is the right time for dancing."

And Melissa got up from the table and went to her room. She came out dressed like a hooker. Arlene told her she might want to cover up a little more. Melissa told her to mind her own business and hurry up with her salad. She was on her way out.

Arlene sat up all night long worried about her sister, Linda. Melissa turned her cell phone off; she called Arlene the next morning telling her how good of a time she had, and that she met this woman. Linda's condition was under control with medication. But Linda had stopped taking her medicine. The medication would make her gain weight. Arlene knew I had to get her back taking her medicine.

Chapter Two

The next day, I called her doctor and told him what was going on. He told me to try and get her to come in. Arlene didn't know how she was going to get Melissa to go to the doctor; she was in control, and now Linda didn't exist anymore. I began to visit Melissa every day, dropping pills in anything she was drinking, until she caught on to what I was doing and dared me at her house. I called the doctor to tell him that she caught me. He knew we had to act fast before Melissa got out of control. I signed papers for Linda to be placed in the hospital. While there, Melissa started seeing one of the ladies she met. This woman had no idea that Melissa's name is really Linda. Melissa was totally different from Linda; she had the personality of a lesbian. She would talk about how attracted she was to this woman. I tried to call out to Linda to see if I could reach her, but Melissa was trying to maintain control, while Donna was also fighting her way to the surface. Melissa knew they planned to put her in the hospital. So she ran away to New York as she planned. Her sister Arlene looked for her all over town, realizing that she was gone. She told the doctor it was his fault. He could have done more to help Linda. And if something happened to her sister, he would be in real trouble. Arlene did not know the first place to look in New York; she was at a loss. She looked for Linda for six months, waiting, and calling all the shelters she could find. One day someone called the number she had given to be reached in case someone knew anything about her sister's whereabouts and told her that she thought the lady living with her ex-girlfriend in Queens may be her sister, but her name was Melissa. I told her that her name was Melissa but we called her Linda and that she needed to talk to her about some family business. The woman asked why I was looking for her. Was she in any trouble? Arlene didn't feel comfortable talking to the lady because there was this strange sound in her voice, as if she wasn't very fond of her sister Linda. Arlene got the address and had to make preparations to go; she knew that she didn't have that much money saved.

She told the doctor he needed to contact the police and let them know that Linda was sick and that we were on the way to pick her up and take her to the hospital. The police asked for her whereabouts; the officer told Arlene that he would keep an eye on her until they got there. By the time we arrived, Melissa had gotten in a fight with her friend, ex-girlfriend. Melissa got in a rage and hit the woman in the head with something. Now the police were involved, and she was in jail. She was in such a rage that she had to be medicated. Melissa was sent to a hospital near home. The doctor told me that Melissa was gone. Donna and Kathy were battling to see who was taking over; the sister I knew as Linda was no more. On some days, I would go and visit my sister but didn't know what name to call her until she began to talk. Donna was quiet; Kathy was generous. I would often call out Linda's name to see if she could hear me. When Linda was in the state of being Donna, she would just sit in the corner of the room looking out into space. Kathy would want to help me do everything. If it was pouring a cup of coffee, she had a baby doll that she carried around with her. She talked to the doll as if it was her baby. My visiting began to slow down when I became sick; I was diagnosed with Alzheimer's disease. There was no one left to take care of Linda, to go and visit her to let her know that she was loved and missed. That worried me more than my own illness. I had always watched over Linda. Early one Tuesday morning, I got a phone call. It was the doctors from the hospital that was taking care of Linda. They were trying some new medications, and they were working. Donna and Kathy were hardly showing up; Linda was back. Arlene rushed to the hospital, to find Linda so medicated that she was worried. Arlene asked the doctor when he last experienced Linda showing up; he told her the previous morning.

"How much medication does she have to take a day?"

"Linda takes at least ten pills a day."

"Are all these pills necessary?"

"Yes."

Arlene told the doctor that she was diagnosed with Alzheimer's disease. He said he was sorry to hear that. He then sat down and made arrangements for Linda in case anything happened to her. Arlene and her sister Linda were very close; they were only four years apart. Arlene's illness started to take a toll on her. Linda woke up asking for her sister, Arlene. The doctor called her sister's house; the nurse answered and told the doctor that Arlene's illness had turned for the worse. She was losing her memory. A nurse had to stay with Arlene; she couldn't be left alone. The doctor got off the phone; he had to think about what to say to Linda to tell her that Arlene was sick. The doctor didn't tell Linda for about two weeks; he wanted to see if her sister's condition would change. The last phone call he made, the nurse told him that Arlene didn't remember anybody. Linda kept asking to see Arlene. Linda knew there was something wrong; she was trying to find her way out of there. She was friends with one of the male housekeepers name Billy; she asked him to please check on her sister and asked if he would give her a message. He asked for the address and went to Arlene's house.

When Billy got there he told the nurse who he was and what he wanted. The nurse told him to come in. She explained to Bill about Arlene's illness, which made him very sad. He knew he would have to go back and tell Linda. Before he left Arlene's house, he did get a chance to see her sister Arlene; she was in her bedroom resting, and he went in.

"Hi, Ms. Arlene, my name is Billy, and I'm a friend of Linda's. She asked me to check on you to see if you were okay. She really misses you, and she asked me to tell you that she loves you and that she is sorry for what she's done."

When Billy was telling Arlene what Linda had said, tears rolled down her face. She touched Billy's hand and whispered, "Tell Linda I love her."

Billy got up and left; he sat in his car for a long time, crying himself. He hated to have to tell Linda how sick her sister really was, but he had to.

The next day, when Billy got to the hospital for work, Linda had been fully medicated. She was crying all night thinking that her sister was dead. Billy told the doctor he had visit her sister, Arlene, and she told him to tell Linda that she loves her, that she was awake, and that she was there for Linda. That evening, Billy went back to Linda's room; she was just sitting looking out of the window.

I called her name; she just sat there. I tried to get her attention; it was if her soul had left her body. This was so sad; the next time I saw Linda there was no Linda to be found. Melissa had come back, never to see Linda again. Billy never got the chance to tell Linda what Arlene told him. The two sisters were separated by illness, never to see each other again.

I MARRIED HIM TWICE

I asked myself, "Is this a form of desperation? Am I in the panic stage? Where are these feeling coming from? Why is my ex-husband Donnie on my mind all the time? I mean, all the good times we shared and the places and people we met. God, what is really going on?"

One evening Donnie and our daughter, Ashley, stopped by the house to pick up some of her things; they were going to the state finals. She played basketball. I couldn't attend this game, and I couldn't get off at the time. He started a small conversation about how life was treating me, but it was something he said. He asked me if I was happy. It wasn't what he asked me, it was the way he asked me. The look in his eyes was lonely. I didn't answer right away; for a moment I went blank.

He said, "Well, are you?"

I said, "It depends. But one thing I can tell you, I am grateful to be alive and well."

He said, "Are you well? You don't have any health issues?"

"No. How about you?"

Donnie said, "I am fine. My health is good, the last time I checked."

"And when was that?"

"Oh, I had a physical two weeks ago."

Donnie yelled for Ashley to come on; it was time to go. We will finish this conversation another time. They got in the car and left. Sunday night, they arrived back home, and he came in. I was ready for bed. I heard Donnie asking Ashley, "Where's your mom?"

She told him I had already gone to bed. He said okay, gave her a kiss, and left. Ashley came into my room and got in the bed with me.

"Mom, are you sleeping?"

"No."

"Mom, can I ask you something?"

"Yes."

"Why did you and Dad divorce?"

"Ashley, we had this talk. Where is this coming from?"

"Mom, all Dad could talk about was our vacations, us growing up, and how much you loved each other."

I sat up in the bed and looked at her.

"Ashley, maybe your dad is going through something right now, and he's down about something. People get depressed sometimes."

"I don't know, Mom, but the way he sounds is like he still loves you. Do you still love him?"

"Ashley, don't start this. It's over between me and your dad. Now stop it."

She jumped out of my bed and ran into her room. I waited for a couple of minutes and went into her room. She was crying. I asked her why she was crying.

She told me, "Because I see you, mom. I see you with your other men friends, and that's just what they are, your friends.

"I know that, Ashley. You're saying that to say what?"

"You don't smile or laugh the way you laughed with Dad." I remember, Mom; there was so much laughter in our house. Then all of a sudden, it was over, no warning, no anything. You and Dad made such a big decision all by yourselves. Did you or Dad stop to think about the way your children would feel?"

"Yes, that's all we thought about. Why do you think he left so quietly? We both were confused; we felt that we lost what we had together. It's so hard to explain what was going on at the time we separated. We lost touch along the way. Somehow, we grew apart. We had stopped talking to each other; his work became primary in his life, and to me it felt like we both went blind. We couldn't see each other anymore."

"Mom, have you ever thought about dating dad again?"

"At first when we broke up that's all I thought about. Did I make a big mistake by telling him to leave? Baby, I really don't know. The more I see him, the more I think about him. Before he wasn't coming in, just picking you up; I could deal with it better. Ashey, try to get some sleep. We will talk more tomorrow."

"Mom, really? I am not going to let you forget."

"I know."

We both went to bed. Ashley got up first and started breakfast. I could smell the bacon. I got up, washed my face and brushed my teeth, and went into the kitchen.

"Good morning, Mom. How did you sleep?"

"Actually, I slept well."

"What about you?"

"Mom, I had a dream. Guess about what. About us—we were a family again."

"Ashley, why won't you just leave this alone? We have been separated for a while now."

"I know, Mom. Something tells me that I'm right."

"What do you mean, you're right? Right about what?"

"You know, Mom. You and Dad getting back together."

"I just don't know what to say to you right now."

"Don't say anything; all I ask mom, is just continue to be open."

Days went by, and one late evening Donnie called. We talked for a while, and the conversation began to get interesting. He asked me if I wanted to go away for the weekend. I asked him where. He said Mexico.

"What makes you think I would go away with you?"

"Well, I don't have anyone special in my life right now, and I don't think you have either. Or am I wrong?"

"No, you're right, but that's no reason to go away with you."

"Well, how about both of us need a getaway, and I really want to talk to you, real talk."

I thought about it and I said, "Why not?"

We both began to laugh. I told Ashley, and you know she told her brother.

I told them, "Don't say anything. It's just a weekend. We agreed that we both need a getaway."

Well, Friday came, and we drove down to Mexico. He booked the hotel room, a real nice room with a view of the beach. The room had two beds. We put our clothes away and went down to the lounge and had a few drinks. Boy, did we laugh about the past and the kids. We talked about his mother and my mom. By the end of the night, we were good and high. I got into my bed, and he got into his. We both fell dead to sleep. He was drunk, and so was I. We got up the next morning. Donnie was up first. He woke me up laughing, standing in the middle of the floor with all his clothes on, realizing that he fell asleep with everything on, and he looked at me with everything off but my shoes. I looked down at myself and began to laugh. We both took turns in the bathroom and got dressed and went to breakfast on the patio by the beach.

That's where all the true feelings came out; he told me about the emptiness he was feeling all this time.

"Yes, I saw other women, but none of them were close. Remember that old saying we had, there's no more me or you. I guess we were right and didn't even know it."

We began to discuss the reasons why we decided to divorce.

He said, "Stop. Wait a minute, Lynn. Let's just take one day at a time from here, today, not worrying about tomorrow, just right now."

I looked at him, grabbed his hand, pulled him close to me, and stuck my tongue so deep in his mouth that he began to do the same. We stopped suddenly for a brief moment, looking each other dead in the eyes. It was as though our souls met all over again, just in a different place and time. He told me that he wants this.

"Please, let's just see what happens."

I told him that I felt him, and it felt so good. We walked back to the hotel to change clothes; we had plans to go see this play at the local town square. The play was nice. It had gotten late; we started back to the hotel. We held hands and talked about how much we enjoyed the evening. We got back to the hotel, and I got in the shower first. By the time I finished, he was sitting on his bed waiting his turn. I had a towel wrapped around me. He passed by me with a big smile on his face. "I see you."

He went into the bathroom and closed the door. I sat on the side of the bed to put lotion on; I had some cute pajamas on, so I got into my bed and turned on the TV.

By the time Donnie got out of the shower, I had fallen asleep. The next morning it was time for us to head home. We laughed, hugged, and kissed. We had decided that we would tell the kids when we were sure that we had a grip on what was going on with us. We arrived home early Sunday, about noon; the kids were both at home when we got there. Donnie took my bags into the house.

Ashley was yelling, "Daddy, how was the getaway?"

"Oh, we had a great time. Right, Lynn?"

"We sure did."

And we both laughed. Ashley and her brother looked at each other, and then turned and looked at us. We smiled, and he put my things down. I told him I would call him later. I went into my room to unpack my things. Donnie lives about an hour away. He talked to the kids before he left to go home. The kids kept asking me to talk about the trip. I told them I was tired, and I would talk to them tomorrow. While lying in my bed, I couldn't stop thinking about the weekend. Fear began to set in, nerves all over the place. I wanted to call him and call this whole thing off. My cell phone rang. It was late, about 11:30 p.m. I answered; it was Donnie.

"Hello, Lynn."

"Hi. Are you still up?"

"Yes. I'm not sleepy yet."

"Neither am I."

He asked where the kids were. I told him David went out. David is our fifteen-year-old son. And Ashley was in her room sleeping.

"Why?"

He said, "Because I wanted to come over. We have some unfinished business."

I said, "What kind of business?"

He asked me to put on some clothes and come over.

"Donnie, I'm already in bed."

"Come on; get up. I promise you I will make it worth your while."

I was scared; I didn't know what to do. I told him we had just left each other, and he was saying that to say what?

"So, come on. Don't think about it; just do it. And that's just what I did. I didn't think about it. I got up, put my clothes on, jumped in my car, and left. When I got to Donnie's house, he was waiting at the door. As soon as I got in the house, he asked me to come into the den. I didn't have the slightest idea where this was going. He had books of pictures out on the floor, pictures of us when we were dating; there was none of the kids, just him and me.

"I didn't know you took those pictures with you."

"Yes, I did. I need something to hold on to."

Boy did we laugh at each other; we both had big hair. Before we realized, it was late

He went and got a pillow and a blanket and asked me where I was going to sleep, on the sofa or in one of the bedrooms. I went and got in his bed. Later that day, I got up. My cell had been ringing off the chain. He told the kids that I was sleeping when they called him, asking if he had heard from me—that you were in your room in the bed when they went to bed.

"I told them I called you and asked you to come over; I told them I would call them back."

"Donnie, is that all you said?"

"Yes. Should I have said something different?"

"No. Boy, I knew they were having a fit. They don't know what's going on. Okay, let's not take this too far."

"Okay, baby, but I had to play with them just a little bit. Hey, Lynn, I got an idea. Let's plan a big dinner at your place, that's the house they grew up in. How about Saturday?"

"I will check to see what their plans are."

Donnie walked toward the kitchen, and I followed him. He took some ground turkey out and fresh tomatoes, basil, and cheese. I asked if he needed some help. He said, "Sure." I asked what he was getting ready to make. "Some pasta," he said. Okay, I took out some mushrooms, green and white onions, and the main ingredient, garlic. He left me in the kitchen to do my thing, and he went to the store for bread and wine. When he got back, we called the kids and told them what we were doing and that I would be home later. Donnie gave me a kiss on my forehead, and we sat down to eat. We had a lovely conversation looking forward, making plans to do things together. I got up to put the dishes away and clean the kitchen, and he got up to help. We played with each other and kissed juicy kisses. It was nice; I told him it was time for me to go home. I left; he said he would call me later. When I got home Ashley and David were all over me.

"Mom, what are you and Dad doing? Are you back together?

"No, no. We are just taking it slow; we know that we are enjoying each other right now, and it feels good.

"Oh, what are you guys doing Saturday?"

David yelled, "Nothing. Why?"

"Well, your dad and I want to have dinner here with you guys. What do you think about that?

"Let's do it," he yelled.

All during the week the kids could not stop talking about it. Donnie and I kept in contact on the phone, having secretive dates besides the ones the kids knew about. Saturday came; Donnie came over, and David and Ashley chose what they wanted for dinner—some meatloaf, garlic mashed potatoes, green beans, and corn on the cob. David and I made banana pudding. Everything was good. Donnie and I had our first real argument. He said something I didn't like, and I called him on it, the way I spoke to him. He said I had so much evil on my face, and I was loud. He told me I don't have to handle him that way—that he wasn't the same person and that he knew how to listen. I told him I was sorry. I felt bad; I had no business doing all that. He said that he didn't realize I took it like that; we got over that just to find ourselves married all over again. We married that summer; Donnie sold his home and moved back into our house. We found ourselves going to our kids' graduation together, not separate, sharing the love that was never lost. This time we both understood what it felt like, for we had shared the same loneliness. It was as if he had never left home. We found ourselves closer, watching how we spoke to each other, and learning each other all over again.

WHAT COLOR AM I?

If you have only 1 percent of African American in you, you're black. African American, please define that for me, Can we really. Is there a pure race in this world we live in? Today's society tells us that if your father is white and your mother is black, you're black, and if your mother is white and your father is black, you're black; 1 percent of black blood makes you an African American. If you really sit down and think about it, something is wrong with that picture. Have Americans created a new bred of people by categorizing us? Shame on us. Yeah, right, shame on you. We as people are so caught up on colors; one thing most people don't want to be is black, a Negro, African American. Why would I say something like that? Since the beginning of time man has stereotyped. Before it was black and white, it was what part of the land or your religion. If you were from a certain part of the land, your skin was brown, and in other parts your skin didn't get very much sun, so your skin color was much lighter.

Growing up I had a hard time identifying myself with other people. What race am I? My father is white, and my mother is black. Everywhere I go I could hear people saying things like, what color is she? She's pretty; her hair is really long, but it's really curly. People can be real cruel. They act like you're not even standing there. Girl, she is mixed; she's not white. She just acts white. Sometimes it sounds like you're some kind of animal. Today there are a lot of mixed marriages; I wonder if the parents ever think about the kids and what they go through. Some parents believe that these kids just might have a better chance in life being of a mixed race, just as long as they are not considered black. What they don't realize is all the jokes being told about them and the fights they get into because we, as a race of people, are never satisfied. It's either you're too black or not black enough. Some black men seek out women of a different race to have babies by, or vice versa, because they don't want their children born black.

Some people of other races seek out blacks to have babies by because they usually are beautiful children, and society accepts them more, and if they are talented it is a plus. Their chances are much greater than being of African descent. Deep inside they feel that an African American is not good enough. They raise their kids around nothing but the white race, teaching them they are better than others. But they still can't erase the fact that if you have 1 percent of black blood in you, you're still considered a black. Now mind you, this is a manmade rule. This is not a fact. The fact is, you are the blood of your father. If your father is white, you're white; if your father is black, you're black; if he is Mexican, you're Mexican. I can go on, but I think you've got the picture. If you notice, on any application they ask for ethnic group or nationality.

I'm forced to choose one of four listed. Being black in the United States is like walking with shadows around you and asking God to please give you some sunlight and free you from the bewilderment. Whatever race is willing to accept a person of whichever blood is so rich; it's rich because it has no room for racism or labels. Our hearts and minds are open to all who are willing to accept us. Sometimes I feel like President Barack Obama. Is the world ready for change, or do they want to continue to hate others because they're different. I asked these questions because one day I would love to have kids of my own.

I am one of the many Americans that have this rare blood that scares everyone. Speaking for the people just like me, with black and white blood running in our veins, we're human just like the rest of you. We live and breathe air; some of you talk about us, anyone with different blood flowing through our veins, like we're not even there.

We carry the blood of the world. If you have mixed parents, your blood has been tampered with. But all of our blood has been tampered with. There is no pure race today. Many you are Negro, Caucasian, Spanish, Italian, African, German, and French, etc. I'm asking America to please help me identify myself; that way I can be added to a race in order for me to complete an application. Just yesterday, I was filling out my college application. When I came to my ethnic group I thought, my father is white and my mother is black. What does that leave me to choose from, anything other than white? If I'm not white, and I'm not, what am I? I'm tired of slapping my father in the face. Wake up. Why do we have to suffer for your fears? It's costing me claiming my father's heritage. Look I have a question, are African American a pure race, you mean to tell me they have no other blood running in there veins. Yeah right, we are living in a world that is fast to legalize gay marriages but that won't let a person claim his or her rightful heritage. We can't because of that zero percent of black blood. What are we really afraid of? The law of the land, this zero percent, as we call it, should be whatever your father is—not mother, but father. Man up, Americans. We as people decided we had the right to love whom every we wanted, and if that meant someone from a different race that what we do. So now what? We know if we bare children their skin would be different. Now your children have to identify their race. Are have we Americans done that for them already. listen to President Obama when he said this is not a White America, Black America, Spanish America, or Asian America; this is the United States of America. I guess it costs too much to be fair. It's cheaper to be a racist.

HE SAVED YOU JUST FOR ME

Chapter One

You run and run, but there is no place to hide. Fears, dreams, confusion, questions unanswered, hate build up in one small person—no one to talk to. Lonely, desperate, and wanting someone to step in, but realizing I'm all by myself. Where do I go from here? At a very young age, I was raped and got pregnant, and that's when my whole life changed right before my very eyes. The man I got pregnant by went to jail, never to see him again. I hated him. My aunt denied the fact that this child was even her husband's, so I moved on. One thing was for sure; it was my baby, and that was good enough for me. Darkened by the fact that I was raped, I still knew not only did the baby have the rapist's blood, but the baby had my blood too. I became not only a mother but a father too. I knew that I wanted my child to grow up educated, proud, strong, and a leader not a follower. I knew I had to get him ready for this cruel world we live in.

So it was just my baby and me. I had no sisters or brothers. That meant I had to lean and depend on myself and the God I served.

I had gotten this job at a local department store, but it was part time, and I had been off for about three weeks. One cold winter morning, I was up to feed Wesley and realized that the lights had been turned off. I knew I was behind on the light bills, but I had to pay the rent. I had no money. My heart began to break; tears ran down my face. Oh, Lord, what am I going to do? I looked around to see if there was anything I could pawn. I didn't have anything good enough; thank God I had powdered milk for the baby.

There's this older man who lived downstairs that is always nice to me. He was always making his way to make sure that I see him in the hall: Good morning. How are you? Can I help you with anything? Maybe I could ask him for help. I went downstairs and knocked on the door. He answered, "Well, hello. Come in.

I told him that I couldn't stay that long. What can I do for you? I began to cry, and he got up and came over.

"It can't be all the bad."

"Yes, it is."

I told him that my lights had just been turned off. He said, "How much is the bill?" I told him, and without any questions he gave me the money, and I thanked him very much. He said it was no problem, and he was glad he was able to help me. I told him that I would pay him back as soon as I could. He said don't worry about it, and to take my time and catch up with the other things I needed to do.

He began to come to my apartment every other day, making sure the baby and I were okay. About seven thirty that evening, I was putting my baby to bed when there was a knock at the door; it was him. I told him to come in. He sat on the sofa, but he had this strange look on his face.

I began to worry. I asked him if everything was all right. He said yes. I went into the kitchen to make some coffee; we both love to drink coffee. As I turned around he was standing there; I asked him again if something was wrong. He said, "I've watched you and your baby ever since you moved into this apartment complex. Your walk is of a proud woman; there always a smile on your face. You say good morning to everyone. I've been living in this complex for twenty years, and some of the neighbors even longer. I can't tell if they have ever spoken to me. They looked everywhere, as if they are afraid to look a person in the face, afraid they just might be forced to speak. The influence that your parents had on you was lasting, because I have never seen such a strong young woman; the things they instilled in you are still alive. It must have taken a lot for you to ask me to borrow money."

"Yes, it did."

My mother always told me that if he brings you to it, he will definitely see you through it. When I found out I was pregnant the first thing that came to my mind was my parents, because they had big dreams for me. After my parents died, I went to stay with my aunt Sarah, but the only problem was Aunt Sarah worked all the time, and that left me at home with her husband and two sons.

Chapter Two

Living with Aunt Sarah was nice for about the first two months; after that, trouble started. My two cousins were horrible teenagers. They were liars, they had guns, and both of them had girlfriends who were tramps. Their girlfriends didn't care that much for me. I was a little on the thin side, and they weren't. We fought all the time. I was in my last year of high school when it became bad.

The boys would try looking at me through my bedroom window to try and catch me with my clothes off. I told my aunt Sarah what they were doing. She said, "Girl, they're just boys." And that was that. They continued. Uncle Tommy, my aunt's husband, would never say too much to me, pretending he wasn't watching me. He drank all the time. No one took Uncle Tommy seriously. Uncle Tommy wasn't the father of her two kids. And her sons reminded him of that all the time. One day while washing my clothes, Uncle Tommy came in the washhouse.

I told him I would be finished in a minute if he wanted to use the machine. He said no. He began to look around as if he was looking for someone. I said, "What's up."

He said, "You know what's up."

He grabbed at me, and the first thing I did was to hit him in his throat so hard and kick him between his legs, and I ran out of the washhouse. I ran to my room and got my clothes, not realizing that we were home alone until he came into my room. He hit me so hard that I passed out. When I came to, everything was already done. I didn't wait for Aunt Sarah to get home. I left. I had no money left from my parents; my aunt had spent it all. She always needed something. She only would buy my school clothes and give me lunch money. My parents left her over my trust fund. The day I ran away I went to try and find my uncle, my mother's only brother, but I had no luck. I had a boyfriend at the time. I called him. We knew I couldn't stay there, so I would wait until late at night when everyone in his house was asleep and stay over there. That lasted for about a week before we were caught. I had to find somewhere else to go. Two weeks later, I began to get sick. I went to the clinic and found out I was pregnant. My boyfriend and I never had sex. Now pregnant for a man that raped me. I told one of the women in the clinic what happened; she told me to call the police and report it. I told her to call my aunt Sarah. She called; my aunt came down to the clinic, and she called me all kind of names and said that her husband would never do anything like that. One of the ladies at the clinic said she was calling the police. Aunt Sarah began to cry. The police picked my uncle Tommy up. He went to jail for a very short time. Here I was pregnant and nowhere to go. One of the ladies at the clinic told me about a halfway house for teen mothers. I went. By the grace of god, they let me finish high school. Time passed, and I got help from a woman named Betsy. She was a woman who ran the women's center. She helped me to find a place to live; the area I lived in I knew I had to leave after the baby was born. There was so much crime; all you heard at night was people screaming and gunshots—just nowhere to raise a child.

Two months after the baby was born I moved to these apartments. I walked with my head high because I knew better. I have hope; I believed in my heart and soul that my condition will change. Change because I am going to fight to make it better. In the nice neighborhood where I grew up there lived a single white woman with two children; she had no husband. I was friends with her daughter. She dressed just as well as I did. Her mother was a nurse. Her children seemed happy. Well, the story goes that when they were younger kids, Maggie was about five and David was seven, their mother got married. She never married their real father. The stepfather had been raping her daughter for two years before her son caught him. She was taking classes and trusting him with her kids; they say her daughter doesn't remember anything. I don't think she does, because she had never talked about it when we were growing up. I often wonder what it was like for Maggie's mother to raise two kids all by herself. She kept a smile on her face; she played with us sometimes. In the morning before we went to school I would come over to meet Maggie, and her mother was at the kitchen table staring out the window. I would ask her what she was looking at. She said, "I am just thinking." Now, today, I find myself staring out the window thinking all the time. What's my next move? What bills are due? Have I made the doctor's appointments for my son? Neither one of us had any idea that I would be facing some of the same challenges she did. Now I know how she did it. She never gave up; she kept moving. There was never a day that passed where she didn't have to figure something out. The next fall I enrolled in a community college not far from my apartment. Wesley had just made two years old, and my neighbor Dwayne, the older man that lived downstairs, and I had become good friends. Dwayne worked nights; he would watch the baby for me sometimes when I went to school. The times he couldn't watch him I stayed home from school. We would take the baby to the park or go to the grocery stores together. He liked to read bedtime stories to Wesley until he went to sleep.

Wesley was very fond of him. Dwayne said that he wanted to talk to me. I told him that I would talk to him after school. I got home from school, put my books down, and when downstairs to pick the baby up. Dwayne had made dinner and asked me to stay and eat. I said, "Sure, I am hungry." After we finished eating I asked him what he wanted to talk about. He began by saying that he enjoyed being with me and the baby and that we had given his life a true meaning. Sitting there saying to myself, "Oh, Lord, where is this going," I began to talk, and he cut me off, saying that he didn't think I would not consider talking to him because he was much older. I told him that it had nothing to do with his age.

"It's just that I am not trying to have any kind of relationship; I haven't seen or talked to a man other than you since my baby was born."

"Don't tell me you're giving up on love."

"Love, Dwayne? I have never been in love. I had only one boyfriend in high school, and when they caught me sleeping at their house when I ran away from my aunt's house that was the end of that.

Dwayne asked me to sit down and calm down. I sat down, and he began to share some things that happened to him in his life.

"You never saw a woman come over my house because I myself had given up on love and on people in general. I had lost hope in people. I had been through many bad relationships, used and abused and anything else you can think of. I was married four years. My wife and I had a little girl. My daughter was a year and a half at the time."

He paused for a moment.

"At what time?"

"The time I came home from work and found my wife in bed with another woman. It was as if I had walked into another world. The next morning she moved out. I would see my daughter off and on until one day the call came that no parent should ever have to answer. She called to tell me that a car had hit my daughter and killed her. So many questions were racing in my head. I was confused, not knowing what to do. Should I kill her mother for not watching her? Don't think that I'm sharing this story with you because I want you to feel sorry for me. I just want you to know that I had my share of ups and downs. I want you to know that you're not alone. I want to take this journey with you. You don't have to be all by yourself. We both know that you're younger, but that does not stop me from feeling the way I do. I'm not afraid to tell how I feel. I'm a man, a real man; I won't run away and leave you. Please trust me. I'll hold your hand when you're scared. I walked our baby to school and back, our baby; I love Wesley too, as if he was my own. Through everything I've gone through, I held on to the desire to love again. I hope that what I told you today does not frighten you. All I ask is that you look at me in a different light. Consider it; don't stop being you. One day at a time is all I ask."

"Dwayne, please don't take this the wrong way, but I wouldn't even know where to begin. I just want to finish my education, buy my dream house, and raise my kid."

Chapter Three

For the first time, Dwayne began to call me by my first name, Ashley. I began to see Dwayne in a different light. Dwayne had a job at an oil refinery, where the pay was good. He began to share his financial status with me. I asked him why. He said he wanted me to know that he lives in these apartments because he chooses to, not because this is the best he can do.

"Ashley, I want to be a part of making some of your dreams come true."

"Dwayne, wait. You are moving too fast for me."

"Okay, I'll back up."

"No, I didn't say back away from me. I just meant slow down a little."

"Ashley, just know I'll be good to you."

That night I couldn't sleep; I tossed all night long, thinking about everything Dwayne had said. Lord, what if this man is the one? But what if . . . Damn the "what ifs." That was driving me crazy. I prayed so hard and asked God to please give me some kind of sign. The next morning I woke up remembering one thing, follow your heart. I was having trouble doing that because my heart was full of hate and shame. Shame of the fact my uncle raped me, and hoping that my son never found out. By the end of the summer, Dwayne and I were in love. We did everything as a family. However, there was one problem. Sometimes I would lose it and say things I didn't mean. Thank God, Dwayne was patient. I knew he was in love with me, and I loved him so much, and he knew it. I ask God to help me with the anger I held inside. In mid spring, we were married. Wesley was old enough to be my ring bearer. I couldn't believe that happiness was only a pray away. All I could think about was my parents, and how happy they were together. God took me back to remind me of my childhood. How happy I was as a kid. After that dream, I felt like I had been born again. When I woke up, I told Dwayne I knew something he didn't. He said, "What?"

"He saved you just for me."

Guess what? I did get the big house with the white picket fence.

MY QUESTION TO GOD

For years I knew that I was different in so many ways. I would always find myself doing things that you would hear grown-ups saying, "Little boys don't do this, and little boys don't do that."

Playing with my friends, especially boys, I had to watch how I would play with them and the things I would say. If I wanted to play with the girls, they would call mea sissy. I would find myself in the circle of girls only because I would like the things they were doing. Growing up, my father and mother always made sure that I was dressed nice and went to a nice school. We lived in a middle-class neighborhood, where your neighbors respected each other. It began in middle school; one boy would always tease me. Sometime he would chase me home. My father would ask me, "Why are you always out of breath running in here? What's wrong? You look like somebody is after you." If he only knew, someone was after me. This boy made it his business to wait for me after school or in the hallways just to embarrass me.

I could not figure out why he hated me so much. Anywhere he would see me, I knew to go the other way because it would be trouble for me. This went on until high school, and something changed. I had my own circle of friends, and he became a loner. In high school I began to find myself being attracted to boys. I wanted to befriend them and get closer, but I was always afraid. I especially admired this really nice-looking senior. But I knew better than to show and act on these feeling. I told my mother how I was feeling. She asked me how long I had felt that way. I told her that I'd had these feeling since the fifth grade.

"Why are you just saying something?"

"Mom, I had to be sure this wasn't something that would go away.

"Are you sure now?"

"Mom, it's the way I see them; when I look at some boys I want to get close to them in an intimate way. Some I even dream about."

My mother got quiet. I asked her if she was all right.

"Yes. You need to tell your dad too."

"I know, mom, but I'm afraid."

"I know, son, but he needs to know."

"I guess he does, but I am not ready to tell him yet. Dad is so gung ho on me being this badass jockey and not worrying about anything else."

"I never heard your dad pushing you to play sports."

"Yeah, and I often wondered why."

"Darrell, your father knows you like to sing and dance." Don't we attend all your musicals?

"Yes."

"Okay. Don't assume anything."

"I guess you're right, Mom. I'm just scared."

"Well, son we don't want him to hear this from anyone else.

"So please don't go telling your girlfriends. I won't be able to get in the school door without everyone knowing my business."

Father came home, and Mom didn't know what to do with herself. Dad asked her why she so quiet.

"Oh, no reason. I was just sitting here thinking.

"What's on your mind?"

She asked Dad questions about what he thought about gays and lesbians. He said they are people just like you and me; some have the same beliefs.

"Do you think that it is a choice?"

"To be honest with you, I believe some gays and lesbians are born different. Their mind tells them one thing, and their body shows something else. Some just simply choose the lifestyle. They enjoy the drama. Mind you, a lot of them are rich and very stable."

My mother said, "So you wouldn't care if you knew the person?"

"What are you talking about? I know people who are gay."

"What if it's your son?"

"Did he tell you he was gay? Has he admitted to you that he is? Has he been with someone? I guess you think I don't pay attention to my son. That's my son, and not to mention my only child. Darrell has been soft from the age of six. Why do you think I never forced him to get into sports? I knew he didn't like football or baseball; he likes to sing, dance, run, and study. I encourage him to sing and study music in college. Now, tell me, did he tell you that he was gay?"

"Yes. So how do you feel about this?"

"I don't know how to feel. I know he is still my son, and I love him. I just don't understand."

"Well, baby, some things are just not meant for us to understand."

"Darrell has to live his own life; I don't believe that he is ready to share this with me."

"Don't let him know that we spoke about this."

His mother went and put her coat on and went to the store. That left Darrell and his father alone. Darrell was in his room, but he could hear his dad on the phone with his friend. They were planning to go fishing over the weekend. Darrell came out of his room, went into the kitchen, and got a glass of water. His dad came in behind him.

"Darrell, I saw you looking at colleges. Have you chosen which school you want to attend?"

"Well, Dad, there are two schools for music and art, but they're located somewhat far away."

"What do you call far?"

"One school is in Atlanta, and the other is in Dallas."

"So, are you afraid to leave home?"

"No, Dad, not really. I just didn't know how you and Mom would feel about me being so far away." "Darrell, there is nowhere on this earth too far to keep us from getting to you if we need to."

Darrell had such a big smile on his face when his dad said that. Darrell felt like it was time to open up to his dad.

"Dad, there is something I need to talk to you about."

"Yes."

"Dad, I don't know how to tell you this, but I have been fighting with this for a long time now."

"What? Son, you can tell me anything."

"Dad, I am gay."

Pausing, he said, "Yes, I know."

"You know. What do you mean, you know?"

"Son, I have watched you grow from a baby until now. You're eighteen years old; I have seen your friends. I watch your mannerisms. I have heard you talk on the phone with your friends and some of your conversations."

"But, Dad, why haven't you said anything?"

"What did you want me to say, that I think my son is gay? I had to wait on you; this is something I had to hear from you."

"Dad, be honest. How do you feel about it?"

"Feel about it? You being gay? Look, son, it's like this. If I told you that I was happy I would be lying. "Disappointed?"

"Yes, a little, only because I need to know if anyone has every touched you. Were you raped?"

"No, Dad, I have never been touched or raped before."

"Darrell, have you chosen this as a lifestyle? Or is this a feeling that you have no control of?"

Darrell took has father's hand and looked him in the eyes and said, "Dad, was I born gay? As soon as I was old enough to like girls, I liked boys instead."

His Dad looked at him with tears in his eyes and said, "I can't tell you that babies aren't born gay. That is a question for God."

"Dad, I wanted to play with the girls, and hoped that the boys wouldn't call me names, they did anyway. Remember when I would come in the house running after school?"

"Yes."

"There were boys chasing me, calling me names. This isn't a lifestyle I chose for myself. This is the way I feel inside; I desire to be with men. I have often wondered why me. In my prayer I have several questions for god: 'Dear God, you know my heart. I come to you as humbly as I know. Why do I have these feeling? Why am I born male and have no feeling for females like a normal man would? This is not a choice of mine. Tell me, God, why? Help me to understand where this comes from. Why do I feel this way? Am I a bad man? I didn't make myself this way, you did. Help me? Does this make me a bad person, nasty? Should I be ashamed? Is this something that I've made up in my mind? Am I sick? Please, God, I need to know. I try hard to live right. In the Bible you speak that women are made for man. Who did you make me for? In Jesus' name, I pray. Amen.'"

His dad could only say and do one thing. He just stood right there with his son holding him, to hear his son pray, cry, and pour his heart out. He wanted his son to know that he and his mother would always love him exactly the way he is. He told his son he did the right thing to pray on it. He told Darrell he wasn't the only person in this world that feels like him. In this world there are so many things that are questionable that none of us has the answer for.

"I know that we are proud of you for trusting in your parents enough to share your feelings, and we respect you for that. I am your father, and I wish I had all the answers, but I don't."

He truly could not answer his questions.

"However, one thing you need to know is that I love you no matter what. You are a kind young man]. Your mother and I only want the best for you; we want you to be happy."

Darrell fell to his knees crying, "Daddy, I would never have thought that you would respond in such a way. I have wanted to tell you this secret for so long. Dad, it feels like a ton of bricks has been lifted off my shoulders. I just want to say that I love you so much; it has always been a fear of mine that you would never accept me being gay."

"It's not about me; this is about you and your life. Now this is between you and God. I hope the questions you prayed to God are answered."

At the beginning of the year I went off the college. There I met new friends and found out that there was more to being gay. Things began to change. The friends I have now are different. Most of them want to be seen, and some don't want anyone to know. Wow, the way gay people separated themselves from others. How gays were getting beaten up; there was talk that two student committed suicide—one hung himself and the other jumped from the top of a building. Boy,

I wasn't ready for this. By the middle of the year things got worse; I was afraid to be myself. Boy, what a life. Wanted to date but didn't have the first clue on how to start a relationship. All I knew was I liked men; I hang with gay people and have yet to find someone who sees me the same way. I still hold my questions for God. (To be continued . . .)

GRANNY'S LOVE

Chapter One

Growing up, there was special little lady in my life who had so much joy about her—her voice, her hugs, even her laughter—oh, and I can't forget her strong hands. She was my safe haven. I knew when I was with my granny, everything was going to be fine. My granny spent a lot of time with me growing up. She was my mother's mom. My mother died of cancer real young, and my granny finished raising me. I had been away for a long time. I arrived late that night, and granny was up waiting for me. We talked a little; she was tired, waiting up for me. I put her to bed and told her I would see her in the morning. The next morning I got up, made breakfast, and sat on the porch. The sunrise was always beautiful. Sitting there, I noticed this car driving by, and this young lady about my age kept looking. She made a U-turn, she came back, and she got out and called me by my name.

"Betty. Betty, is that you?"

"Who's asking?"

"Betty, it's me, Tammie."

"Tammie."

I jumped up and ran off the porch.

"Tammie, how are you? I haven't' seen you in years."

"I know. Where have you been, Betty?"

"Girl, I moved years ago. I've been gone twenty years now."

"Girl, you looked good."

"Well, thank you. You don't look so bad yourself."

"Betty, what happened? One day I came to Granny's house to see you, and she said you had packed up and left, in search of a better life."

"Tammie, between drugs, men, and no job, I was done. I got clean before I left here. That's when my eyes were truly open; I could see all the hurt and pain I was placing on myself and my grandmother. I couldn't believe how bad it had gotten. Thank God for praying grandmothers. She taught me how to pray and told me about God and his forgiving heart, and how much he loved me. So I reached out to him for myself, and here I am today, a changed woman because of him. I really want to give God all the glory and praise because through him I became a new me."

"Well, what brought you back down here, my granny?"

"Tammie, I came home every year during Thanksgiving. I didn't even see you. I know because you don't go to the same church as Granny, and that's the only place I go when I am here. Tammie, there's one thing I learned for sure; leave all the old things in the past where they belong, drugs, drinking, and men. Anything that had to do with drugs or someone on drugs has no place in my life. The new me—don't do drugs, don't smoke and drink—with a clear mind, and I do exactly what I want. I've set goals for myself, and half of them I have already accomplished."

Tammie looked at me and said, "Well, I guess you're too good for us now. What does that mean, you know, what you just said, anyone on drugs or drink they can't be a part of life?"

"Okay, I did say that. Are you telling me you're still using?"

"Yes, sometimes."

"Tammie, it's all up to you."

"What you want to do?"

"The things you do, I don't do anymore. You know what, let's talk about this later. And I have to take Granny to the store."

Tammie gave me her number and asked me to call her later. I went into the house to see if Granny was ready to go to the grocery store.

While driving, I could see the neighbors out, some standing on the corner—abandoned houses, drugs being sold on the corners. Kids Park was already taken over by local gangs. The neighborhood was a mess. Granny told me that she has her groceries delivered to her. I began to talk.

She said, "Betty, I know you don't miss any of that."

"Granny, I think it was the last time I got down on my knees to pray. I asked God to remove the cocaine habit from me, and I said I would never ever do it again. Granny you always told me, when I talk to the Father, call it out by name. I never stop praying. I began to stop smoking and drinking on my own, and one day I realized that I had been delivered from all my bad habits. He started from the smallest and worked his way down, and in his time and terms. His terms were me asking him. It was just this easy."

Chapter Two

The next evening, Granny shared something with me. She told me that this young lady at her church had been going through so much, she was down on her luck, and her faith was being tested.

"I hope you don't mind, baby, but I told her your testimony. After I shared your story with her, she had hope again. I hope you don't mind?"

"No, Granny, if sharing my testimony with anyone will somehow help them or lift them up. That's just another form of proving how great God's power is, and how much he really loves us. What the word says, Granny, ask and you shall be given, knock and the door will be opened. Simple as that!"

I had two days before I would be leaving town, and I called Tammie and asked her if she wanted to join me and my grandmother for dinner. She said yes. That night after dinner, Tammie and I sat on the front porch with hot cups of tea, and I began to share the word with her. At first she had all these ifs and buts. I stopped her and asked her if she was really ready to listen; she finally gave in. I began by telling her she was in a battle.

"In your heart you know what's right, but you have a strong desire for drugs and everything of the world. We realize that the soul and the flesh are two different things. The flesh is only temporary, but your soul is forever.

"It's where we want our soul to remain after the flesh is gone, Heaven or hell. The choice is yours. I went around thinking that I couldn't enjoy my life if I was a Christian, that a Christian's life is boring, but I am happier than I have ever been. When I was in the world, I never had a peaceful day, high, always looking and trying to figure out where I was going to get my next high from, not my next meal, but the next high. Running from drug dealers, couldn't pay my bills, selling my body. It was horrible. I can truthfully say that living in Christ, none of that exists anymore. I see things differently; everything good is of God. I want you to always remember that. In this life God allows us to go through certain things to learn from.

"I challenge you to let go of those old ways and allow God to step in, and watch the light begin to shine in. Doors begin to open that you never knew you would even have interest in. Christ has bigger and better plans for you. Just open up and let him in. Look at me, Tammie. I am a living witness. I love who I am now. Yeah, some of you know the old Betty, and I can't change that. That's my past; the pass is exactly what it is. It doesn't pay me to be embarrassed about it because it's my testimony and where I come from, and with my testimony I can tell you that you don't have to live like that. Give your life to Christ and watch the new Tammie unfold. I am a living witness and he has the same love for you."

I went into the house and got my granny. I asked her to pray with us. Before we began, Granny asked Tammie if she wanted to start, she said no. Granny took our hands and began to pray.

I opened my eyes, and I could see the tears running down Tammie's face. I told the devil she didn't belong to him and to release her in the name of Jesus. Granny began to speak in tongues, right outside on the porch. Tammie opened her eyes for the first time and saw who she really was. She was asking God to please forgive her for the way she was living. I told her it's already done. The next morning, I left and returned home. Two weeks later Granny called me and told me that Tammie was coming to church regularly. Well, that's a start; my granny told me how proud she was that I took the time out to help a friend. No, Granny, thank you for never turning your back on me and for never letting me give up.

RUN AND TELL THAT

I work at a predominantly black company with lots of so-called professional people. Yeah, right, start by saying bull shirt. I have never seen so much bitterness in my life. Some people are filled with so much hate. Why? Just because they can. You tell me they don't even know. They try and find the smallest thing to nitpick about, or god forbid you were to make a mistake. It's on. Just as long as they are making you feel bad and looking down on the other person, they have fulfilled their task for that day. Running and telling anything that might belittle, or trying to make folks lose their jobs, and get in the way of promotions. They choose the people around them who are mad at the world or unhappy for one reason or another to team up with; I mean people with high positions are involved in some of this, and with all the bad rumors, you are surely doomed. People, they call it the clique, a bunch of haters.

Most of the time the person they're hating on has never done anything. They don't even know they're being hated on. Haters even try and befriend you just to find out things about you, just so they can gossip in hopes of getting the news to the grapevine. The grapevine consists of the people who share gossip, and people who go around sharing rumors and hating on other folks. This is what makes them feel better. They're the big person now. They enjoy the hype. Oh, yeah; they only discuss the negative things, nothing promising for you—no, that's too much like right. You don't hear the hater talking about that other haters in their clique, who is in the closet, the ones who is sleeping with the same sex. Who knows what some of them are hiding. They don't because they're in the clique. Remember, keep the focus off them. **Run and tell that.** Those haters never stop to think about the person, the victim. The victim usually gets used to the behavior and tolerates it. Some walk with a big smile on their face, go home, and come back to the workplace with two or three guns, and maybe even more, and shoot up the place. They have cried, yelled, and run away, until nothing is left but a smile. Sometimes I used to sit down and wonder why. I don't anymore; I realize that I was that important. Who else more exciting than me? I really don't know anyone else. I mean, I love myself, and I love people, love to laugh and have fun. Oh, and I forgot to mention I love men. Some of my coworkers love to see me coming, men and women. They know that they are going to do one or two things—laugh out loud; believe me, they will be smiling before I leave them. Sometimes I sneak and share sex stories with them; I have them just about on the floor laughing. Some people say I missed my calling; I should have been a comedian. I love making people laugh. I get true joy out it. Some of the women admire the clothes I wear; some of the witches think I'm crazy. I know they don't mean me any good.

When I pass them in the hallway, "you look nice" in one breath and calling me a B in another. But what they don't know is, I've already identified them from the time I saw them standing there waiting for me to pass. Whatever, hater. Most of you are lonely, with no man and no toys either. **Run and tell that.** They hate to see me coming, but not the men and some of the women. The women that know who they are and are not afraid to show it with confidence, we always greet each other. Most of the men roll out the red carpet; they have such a big smile on their faces when they see me coming and, boy, do I get a kick out of that. Most of them ask me not to change. "You are so pleasant." Some of them say, you just made my day; when I saw you coming with that big smile, I couldn't wait to say hello. You don't walk around with your nose in the air like you're better than others. Don't ever stop smiling and being you. You always dress professionally, and you never pass anyone without speaking."

I am glad my parents believed in addressing others when you enter the room or in passing. Some folks turn their heads to keep from speaking; now that's doing too much. Time went on in the workplace, and I had hope that things would get better, but that wasn't the case at all. The hating got worse. I found myself in the middle of hell, sometimes wanting to tell somebody about all this evilness at work but not knowing who to talk to. This is a big world but yet so small. Trying to talk to anyone at work is like telling the hater what they're doing is working. You try not to take it home with you. You find yourself just wanting to be held by your spouse. What about the ones who don't have spouses? They hold on to the ugly things that have been done to them that day, and they feel miserable. Born with a soft heart, you always try to find the good in people. That's where I went wrong. The haters go home talking about me to their spouses.

Now the spouse is calling the job with attitude, asking to speak to his or her spouse. But, my thing is, you don't know what part your spouse is playing at work. I mean, you think they are just sitting there doing nothing. Some of them don't care, because they don't wear the pants at home anyway. Their wives are the breadwinners. So that makes him yes men anyway. Yes, they are the one who throw rocks and hiding their hands. Their lips are so fat and juicy from kissing so many butts, because their skills are useless. Yeah, a lot of you haters used to do a lot of things; you can't anymore. Don't hate; just step aside. You had your turn. Many spouses just listen to that the stories they come home with,, they already know their spouses are hating. They sit their fat asses up and let themselves go; now they are mad at the world. You haters need to leave the young people alone. Let them do their thing; you used to do yours.

At first, you wonder why some people try so hard to get in your mix, when they barely had one word to say to you before. I mean, they eat lunch with you and invite you to places, and they can't wait to get to work and tell everybody what went on. All I had to do was stay friends with them long enough until the truth exposed itself. They're trying to find out who you are sleeping with. Is it someone at work? Surely, the person trying to find out all this mess is the main one that's doing all sorts of things with everybody; just trying to keep the focus off them. If they keep people's focus on you, then no one realizes how much of a tramp they really are. **Run and tell that.** Some people let themselves get to a place of so much hate, fear, low self-esteem, and no confidence in themselves, and they blame everyone else. They target people with a warm smile who greet people, someone with a kind word. Those are the ones they try to break down.

I say to all you haters, keep hating, go on and talk about me. Keep me in your heart and minds; I hope I am the first thing on your mind when you get up in the morning and the last thing when you go to sleep at night. I hope you go home telling your husbands and wives about me so your husband or your wife can dream about me. wishing for the same confidence. Keep coming to work trying to steal my joy. At the beginning you almost had me, until I realized that I have never really done anything to most of them. I mean, yes, I had to back some of you off me. Other than that, you are just hating. So as long as you are hating, I will continue to be blessed by the things you haters whisper in your friend's ears. You know, the negative stuff, distorting the way other people look at me. I don't think so; keep whispering "Lord have mercy" every time you see me coming, or bless her soul. Continue to ask the lord to bless my soul and have mercy on me. For the hater out there that continues to hate on coworkers who are just trying to have a decent eight hours of work, just know this, if they spend their time trying to figure out what your problem and why you're hating, they will take away from the things that they enjoy doing and what makes them smile. And that's not going to happen. And as for me, so long as you're hating, for whatever reason, I laugh and continue smiling. You know, that smile you hate so much. You're probably afraid that your man or woman might say something to me. He or she probably already has. Don't be mad.

I will continue to dress to impress, and may it do what it does. After all, it is what it is.

You Feel Me. **Now run and tell that.**

GIVING THANKS

I would like to thank my family and friends for their support, my adopted families that I gain along the way, and all of you who welcome me in your homes and hearts willfully. To my two sons, Willie Brisco Sr. and Kenneth Cormier Jr., I would like to thank you for always believing in me through the hard times and the good times, for always keeping your chin up, for the love we share, and for the friendship. I wouldn't change a thing. I must say I am truly blessed to have such great sons. I want you both to know that I am proud of the men you have become; just know that God is not through with you yet.

ABOUT THE AUTHOR

I'm a person with a flight of ideas, who was born and in raised in a small town in Texas called Port Arthur, a part of the Golden Triangle. It's surrounded by the Gulf of Mexico; this city is known as the city that oils the world. Port Arthur has more than fifteen major oil refineries. Folks were sure this town would blow up one day; some called it Lil Chicago. Whenever there was a bad accident at one of the major oil refineries they would set off this alarm; the sound of the alarm was so loud you could hear it all over the city. People knew something bad had happened, and we might have to evacuate.

In junior high school, I could watch the ships pass through the gulf canal out of my classroom window. There was an older man who would swim in the gulf canal; the students always thought one of the ships would take him under and drown him, but it never did. Instead, he just died of old age.

Growing up, there were so many floods. We would wait until the rain stopped and go outside and play in the water, like we were in a swimming pool. Yes, the water was dirty, but not so dirty you couldn't play in—not to us anyway. Just a lot of rainwater from the ditches and overflowing canals, and things of that nature. A lot of the families went to the large schools for shelter. Most of the people I knew and grew up with are gone; some have yet to leave. I have two beautiful sons. My oldest son was born on my father's birthday, and my youngest son on the day after my mother's birthday. Just can't beat that.

My mother and father died in the early part of my life, never to meet their beautiful grandchildren. My father was killed in a bad traffic accident; one of my brothers was on the back of the motorcycle when it happened, and my mother was driving the car behind them with my other brother with her. They saw everything, and, to top that off, it was on Mother's Day.

Four years later my mother passed from a broken heart; she was so lonely. She didn't want another husband; she wanted to be with her husband, the man that won her heart years ago. There have been many tragedies in the Brisco family. Maybe one day I'll write about it, but for the most part I loved growing up with my sisters and brothers; we lost our younger brother in 2002. We miss him so.

Growing up we had a vacation every summer, and my mother would plan everything. My father would show off in front of us, telling us he had been all over the world, and narrating the entire trip. I was always told growing up that I look like my father.

As a young girl I was a dreamer; my parents said I was born with a veil over my face. That meant you could see things, before it happened. Sometimes when I had dreams my mother would take me over to my Aunt Minnie's house, and she would always tell us what the dream meant, but that's another story.

I have always wanted to step out and do something different—become a movie star, a singer, a dancer; anything that had to do with bright lights and cameras, that was me. Our mother was a very good dresser, and so was my older sister. She taught me everything about makeup and dressing up, and I thought she was the prettiest girl I had ever seen. Daddy used to tell me, "Girl, you act like you were born with a silver spoon in your mouth." When my parents would take us school shopping, I would always ask for the highest-priced clothes in the store. I didn't get them, but I tried anyway.

My youngest sister was born on my older sister's birthday. She was so chubby and pretty; her hair was long and curly. The neighbors would ask my mom to brush my baby sister's hair, sometimes she would. You see, my life growing up wasn't always happy times, but I must say that until I lost my parents, life was good as I knew it.